Should McKennas act on their feelings, they will put their loved ones in mortal danger....

He didn't want to think he was falling for the woman. His heart was elsewhere, right?

He kept seeing Grace. Entering his office. At the fundraiser. In his arms. She was staring at him now, wide-eyed, as if she could read his mind. Which probably she could if she touched him. No more touching, he thought.

What if he fell for Grace?

The curse...he'd already acted—

It wasn't too late, Declan assured himself. All he had to do was keep from falling for her and she would come out of this all right.

At least she would be alive.

PATRICIA ROSEMOOR

SAVING GRACE

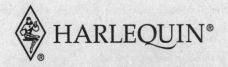

HARLEQUIN®

TORONTO • NEW YORK • LONDON
AMSTERDAM • PARIS • SYDNEY • HAMBURG
STOCKHOLM • ATHENS • TOKYO • MILAN • MADRID
PRAGUE • WARSAW • BUDAPEST • AUCKLAND

Thanks as always to the members of my critique group—
Sherrill Bodine, Rosemary Paulas, Cheryl Jefferson,
Jude Mandell and Laurie DeMarino—
who brainstormed with me through the tough spots.

Recycling programs
for this product may
not exist in your area.

ISBN-13: 978-0-373-74521-0

SAVING GRACE

Copyright © 2010 by Patricia Pinianski

This edition published by arrangement with Harlequin Books S.A.

For questions and comments about the quality of this book please contact us at Customer_eCare@Harlequin.ca.

® and TM are trademarks of the publisher. Trademarks indicated with ® are registered in the United States Patent and Trademark Office, the Canadian Trade Marks Office and in other countries.

www.eHarlequin.com

Printed in U.S.A.

ABOUT THE AUTHOR

Patricia Rosemoor has always had a fascination with dangerous love. She loves bringing a mix of thrills and chills and romance to Harlequin Intrigue readers. She's won a Golden Heart from Romance Writers of America and Reviewers' Choice and Career Achievement Awards from *RT Book Reviews*. She teaches courses on writing popular fiction and suspense-thriller writing in the fiction writing department of Columbia College Chicago. Check out her Web site, www.PatriciaRosemoor.com. You can contact Patricia either via e-mail at Patricia@PatriciaRosemoor.com, or through the publisher at Patricia Rosemoor, c/o Harlequin/Silhouette Books, 233 Broadway, New York, NY 10279.

Books by Patricia Rosemoor

CAST OF CHARACTERS

Grace Broussard—The model for a New Orleans clothing designer fears a blackmailer will ruin not only her career but those of her politician mother and brother.

Declan McKenna—The private investigator soon finds reason to get closer to his new client.

Raphael Duhon—Have the designer's money troubles driven him to blackmail?

Max Babin—The photographer has access to the dressing room where the hidden camera photographed Grace.

Eula Prejean—A security guard. Is she covering up what she knows about Grace's situation?

Bergeron Prejean—The brother of the security guard. He's been banned from the building.

Helen Emerson—What would she do to take the judge's seat from Grace's mother?

Jill Westerfield—She seems ready to do anything to get ahead.

Larry Laroche—The politician has a reputation for ruining his opponents.

June 22, 1919

Donal McKenna,

Ye might have found happiness with another woman, but your progeny will pay for ths betrayal of me. I call on my faerie blood and my powers as a witch to give yers only sorrow in love, for should they act on their feelings, they will put their loved ones in mortal danger.

So be it,
Sheelin O'Keefe

Chapter One

She was the most stunning creature he'd ever seen.

The raven-haired woman entered through a door that should have been locked. It was well after ten. Behind her, the street was muted with fog that curled over the pavement and up the streetlights. Declan McKenna stood frozen at the front desk of Vieux Carré Investigations and let the stapler he'd just picked up tumble from his fingers back to the desktop.

"I need you," she said, her low, throaty voice sizzling down his spine.

"Then have me. I'm yours."

A perfectly arched brow revealed her annoyance with his attempt at humor. "I need your services," she amended. "Your *professional* services. You *are* a private investigator?"

"Forgive me. You took me by surprise." He straightened. "Declan McKenna, one of the owners of Vieux Carré Investigations." His cousin and partner, Ian, was out of town, the reason Declan had spent all night wrestling with paperwork. They didn't have any other employees, not while they were working to get the business in the black, so they had to do everything from footwork to accounting.

"I'm Grace Broussard."

Declan moved to his office door and held out an arm to invite her in. "Please."

Closing the outside door, she stepped forward.

What an eyeful she was in a sleek black dress, both sides slitted to reveal glimpses of long, long legs. Her raven hair dusted her shoulders and came to a peak at her waist. There was something familiar about her, but he couldn't quite place where he'd seen her before. Mesmerized by the length of Grace's spine as she moved into the office before him, Declan removed his jacket.

She was making him sweat.

Grace took a seat, and Declan rounded his desk, one of the many antiques adorning the office. Not Declan's taste. Not Ian's, either. They'd bought the business, lock, stock and furniture, from the previous owner. The decor was appropriate for a business situated in the French Quarter, so they hadn't changed anything, not even the dark green paint on the walls.

Declan hung his jacket on the back of his chair and sat. "What can I do for you, Ms. Broussard?"

"Grace, please. I need you to find out who's been following me."

"What makes you think you're being followed?"

Not that he disbelieved her. Most likely more than one man had followed her at some time or other.

"Let's say my senses are sharp, in tune with my surroundings. I've been aware of someone following me several times in the past two weeks."

"Did you see who?"

"No, but I'm not imagining it. I thought perhaps it was a fan. But then there are these." She opened her purse and pulled out several folded sheets of cream-colored paper. "The first came in the mail at work."

Unfolding one of the missives, she placed it on the desk and slid it toward him. He stared at the words printed in caps.

I'VE BEEN WATCHING YOU

She placed the second sheet on top of the first. There was a little hitch in her voice when she said, "The second message was delivered to me at a social gathering. A charity dinner. I found it under my plate."

I SEE EVERYTHING YOU DO

"And now there's this, pushed under my apartment door sometime during the night. Or maybe that's what woke me up so early this morning."

Her hand was shaking now as she smoothed out

the final note. Declan stared at the four words printed neatly in the middle of the third missive.

I CAN EXPOSE YOU

"Do you know what the threat means?" he asked.

"It must have something to do with my work."

"Which is…?"

"I represent a new line of designer clothing called Voodoo."

Declan snapped to and felt a flush creep up his neck as he placed her—that ad in the New Orleans *Times-Picayune*. Her lying across a red satin-covered bed, back arched, arm lazily thrown over her head, the words under the photo: Voodoo…Put A Spell On Him Tonight….

He'd wanted the woman in that ad to put a spell on him!

Clearing his throat, he said, "Sounds like this could be a stalker. Have you been to the police?"

"No police," she said. "Not unless absolutely necessary."

"Tell me why."

Grace took a big breath. "Bad publicity could be devastating to my mother's career. She's an assistant district attorney and slated to fill a judicial vacancy. And then there's my brother, a city council member up for re-election. I wouldn't be able to bear it if I somehow ruined the lives of the people I love."

As a man who believed in family loyalty, Declan was impressed. Grace's emotions were raw, right on the surface. A person didn't have to be an empath to read her. But as a McKenna, he could do so more quickly and more deeply than the average person. All the members of his family had some native ability—his being able to read anyone's emotions.

"So, I gather you'd like us to provide you with a bodyguard."

"No!" Her depthless gray eyes widened. "I can't have someone following me around every moment. I want you to figure out who this pervert is and help me find a way to dissuade him from doing anything I would regret."

"To find him, I would have to dig into your life. You need to realize an investigation sometimes brings to light things people would rather see stay buried."

"I have no skeletons in my closet," she said firmly, but suddenly she couldn't seem to meet his gaze.

"And your family?"

"Of course not!" she snapped.

Making him certain she was hiding something. Well, that made two of them. Not that either his McKenna gift or the McKenna curse had any bearing on the case. He'd abandoned the woman he'd fallen for before anything serious could happen between them. The last time he'd seen Lila Soto, one of the serious artists his sister Aislinn represented in her gallery, her spirit had been crushed, and her dark eyes had been deep pools of pain— pain that he'd caused even though he'd left his home in New Mexico to protect her.

Grace Broussard was exactly the kind of woman he used to go for. Grace was gorgeous and sexy, but she was no Lila. Not soft and shy and funny and generous. Not the type of woman to whom he would ever give his heart.

"So you would be comfortable with whatever background information I learn about you or your family."

"As long as you keep to a confidentiality agreement."

Declan nodded. "Of course. All right, I'll take the case. We charge eight hundred a day plus expenses."

"Agreed."

Declan had Grace fill out some paperwork and sign a waiver so that he had permission to dig where he saw fit. When she was done, a rush of something he couldn't quite name shot through him as he held out his hand to shake on the deal.

A FEELING OF HELPLESSNESS—as though she were rushing to some inexplicable destiny—came over Grace. A sound like white noise filled her head and she found herself staring into thick-lashed green eyes with deep lids at half-mast. Bedroom eyes.

Forcing herself to concentrate, she stretched out her hand. Declan's long fingers wrapping around hers shot a rush of heat through her and sizzled along her nerves. Shocked, she felt the room narrow as an image quickly flipped through her mind....

Declan tears off his tie...catches her by the hips and runs his lips along her naked spine....

Spine tingling from neck to hips, Grace smothered a gasp and tried to look natural as she freed her hand. It *couldn't* be happening to her again...not after all these years. Good Lord, what had she just done?

Her imagination was playing tricks on her. She hadn't really seen what she'd thought upon touching him. Not possible, because she didn't have visions anymore.

Not even by accident!

"I'll need you to leave the notes," Declan said. "And I would like to get your fingerprints so I can eliminate them when I run my tests on the paper."

His stare was so intense she could feel it all the way down to her toes. As if *he'd* read her mind, his full mouth quirked into a grin, stretching the faint scar on his chin.

"Fingerprints...but that would only incriminate someone who'd already had their fingerprints taken. A criminal."

"Chances are, that's exactly who we're dealing with."

"Right."

"Don't worry, we won't have to mess up your fingers with ink. My cousin is an electronic junkie. Even though we're a small business, he has to have the latest tools, including one for electronic fingerprinting. I'll be just a moment," he said, leaving the room.

Great. Fingerprinting. That meant Declan would touch her again. Ten times. Once for each finger. Ten more chances to flash on some nonexistent future.

But when he came back and set the equipment on the desk before her, he said, "You just need to press each finger to the screen, one at a time. It'll only take a few moments."

Relief washed through her when she realized Declan didn't have to touch her again, after all. As she followed his instructions, Grace knew that she needed to get hold of herself, stop imagining the unthinkable. Get her mind back to the problem at hand.

"I need some basic information," Declan said. "About your place of business and the people you work with."

Though she couldn't imagine the stalker was that close to her, Grace said, "Raphael Duhon is the owner-designer of Voodoo. And Max Babin is the photographer he uses. I really don't work with anyone else on a regular basis."

"You're on good terms with both of them?"

"I am. Raphael actually owns the building where both Voodoo and Gotcha!, the photography studio, are located. It's at Decatur and Iberville."

"All your shoots are inside, then?"

"No, not all. I'm also the spokeswoman for Voodoo, so I do a lot of society and charity events. I'm constantly being photographed at them."

"That complicates things. Some man you met at one of these functions could have targeted you. When's the next event?"

"As a matter of fact, I have one tomorrow night."

"Do you have an escort?"

"No—"

"You do now. I can scope out the people around you with a fresh eye. If anyone has taken an unnatural interest in you, I'll spot him."

They made plans to talk later—they would pick a place to meet then. Grace left Vieux Carré Investigations and headed for home with a lighter heart than she'd had when she entered.

Even so, as she walked down the street, she couldn't help but look over her shoulder. If some dangerous man lurked behind her, she couldn't spot him. Declan McKenna would have a better eye for these things than she did, the reason she'd hired him.

Even so, she walked faster.

She'd never been afraid before—not like this, not on so many levels.

For once in her life, she had something she could call her own—an actual career that she loved. She'd done a lot of searching, had gotten off to a lot of bad starts, but finally—finally!—she knew what she was meant to do.

Being photographed wasn't important to her, though she did enjoy it. Being able to draw on the contacts she'd made all her life to help break out a talented designer and to raise donations for various charities through her appearances meant a great deal to her. It gave her a purpose in life she'd never before had. She could follow family tradition, but in her own unique way. In the past, she'd endured society functions. She hadn't fit in. Now she saw them as a way to use her celebrity to do good for folks who needed help. It was a win-win situation for everyone involved.

For the first time, she was really happy with her life.

Now someone was trying to ruin that, to take the joy she'd finally discovered from her work. Grace wasn't about to let that happen, no matter what she had to do.

Or see, she thought, remembering the vision she'd had when touching Declan.

No, no. It wouldn't happen again, she assured herself, remembering the traumatic incident the last time she'd used her ability.

Never again.

She was so focused on her distraught thoughts that she didn't realize she'd automatically taken a shortcut down a narrow side street—one that wasn't well lit. The area seemed deserted…but the hairs on the back of her neck stood at attention.

Was she being followed?

This time when she turned around, she spotted a dark figure slip into a doorway.

Heart hammering, trying not to panic, she sped up.

Footsteps slap-slapped behind her, quickly drawing closer. Nearly choking on her breath, she pushed herself, now running blindly in her panic. The threatening footfalls echoed through her head and she feared her pursuer was nearly upon her….

A door opened and she ran into a tall, broadly built man exiting and lost her balance.

He caught her before she fell. "Easy, chér." His expression concerned, he looked behind her. "Is there a problem?"

Grace looked, too, but whoever had been following her had melted into the night.

"Sorry, I got turned around and didn't know where I was," she lied. "The hour is so late…" Nearly midnight. "The street's empty…I just got scared."

The young man grinned. "Would you like us to walk you home?" He indicated a woman who'd followed him out of the building.

Relief washed through her. "I would be so appreciative. I'm in the Marigny, just the other side of Esplanade."

"No problem. Anything for a lady."

Feeling infinitely better, Grace gave the empty street behind her one last searching look.

SO NOW WHAT WAS Grace Broussard up to, going to a private investigator? Did she really think she was going to get out of this?

Of course she did.

Privileged people never thought bad things could happen to them. They assumed that while they wreaked havoc on other people, they could go through life unscathed. That they could do whatever they wanted, whenever they wanted, and that they would never have to pay.

Grace Broussard was about to learn different.

The stakes just went up…

Chapter Two

"Minny, what are you doing here?" Grace asked when she arrived early for her shoot the next morning and found her cousin wandering around Gotcha!

The photography studio wasn't open this early. There was no one currently on hand to stop anyone from coming through. The last receptionist had been let go the week before—Max said Eva just wasn't working out, but Grace had overheard an argument between Max and a supplier about cost, making Grace wonder if finances were the real reason.

Minny had made herself at home.

"I was looking for you, of course, Grace. So what do you think?"

Minny was posed in front of the scrim, lit with a pale lavender—the only soft thing about the scene. Minny's hair glowed red. Not auburn, not mahogany, but a stoplight red that made her freckles pop. Her floaty blouse was a pattern of red and gold, and she wore gold capris.

Nothing subtle about Cousin Minny.

Wondering where Max had gotten to—since the lights were on, the photographer was obviously in the middle of setting up for the shoot—Grace echoed, "What do I think? It all depends on what you want to advertise."

"My business, of course." Minny waved red-tipped fingers heavy with rings of garnets and topaz. "I was thinking of running a big ad in the *Times-Picayune*."

For the past several years, Minny had run a shop in the French Quarter where she read palms and auras and tarot. Of course she used her gift to get the goods on the customers, so her predictions always rang true.

Grace thought to tell Minny about the spooky notes—about someone following her the night before and about her hiring a private investigator—then thought again. She trusted Minny implicitly—perhaps the only person she could say that about. While normally her cousin would keep her confidence, Grace wasn't sure she would when it came to her being threatened. The last thing she wanted was for Mama or Corbett to know that someone was stalking her and that she'd hired a professional to resolve the situation.

Scrubbing the situation from her mind so Minny couldn't use her psychic abilities to catch on, Grace said, "If you're serious about needing a professional photo, I'll talk to Max—"

"Nah, I'm just thinking about it. Don't know if I'll ever do it. I'm the shy type, not like you, Grace."

"Yeah, sure," Grace said with a laugh.

Minny had always put herself right out there, ever since Grace could remember. Her cousin had never had the trouble using the family *gift*.

"Why don't you come back to the dressing room with me? I have a shoot scheduled in an hour—a new line of Raphael's lingerie."

"Ooh, let's see. I just *know* it'll be the real me."

One of the few people who knew the real Minny Broussard—her cousin acted her way through life—Grace laughed and led the way back to the dressing room. Even though the woman used to babysit her, they'd gotten along as contemporaries for years.

"So what do you need from me?" Grace asked, as she shed her clothing for a filmy robe.

"Need?" Minny echoed. "Can't I simply stop by to see my favorite little cousin?" Minny touched the side of Grace's face and looked deep into her eyes.

Grace ducked and started on her makeup. "Don't be coy," Grace said, using the mirror to watch Minny check out the skimpy lingerie hanging on the clothing rack. "You're up to something. What happened?" Wanting to distract her cousin if she'd somehow sensed the stalker issue, Grace asked, "You somehow got the S-O-S on my psychic slip?"

"You slipped? Well, isn't this an interesting development."

Grace stopped what she was doing and turned to face Minny, who was studying the first thing Grace would model—a delicate black bustier laced with magenta ribbons.

"Declan McKenna isn't my type, Minny," Grace said, believing it even as she saw him in her mind's eye and her pulse picked up a beat. "So don't make this into a thing."

Minny pulled the hanger holding the corset from the rack. Seeming extra-intent, she gazed at the garment, then used her free hand to touch it. For a moment, Minny's expression deepened into a frown that made the flesh along Grace's spine crawl.

"What?" Grace demanded, her voice strained, knowing her talented cousin could get psychic readings from objects, as well as from people.

Minny shook her head, but her expression didn't lighten. "Something strange…*bad vibes*…can't quite get it. Maybe you shouldn't wear this."

As if she didn't want to touch the bad vibe bustier any more than necessary, Minny set the hanger back on the garment rack and separated it from the other designs.

"A fancy bustier is giving you bad vibes?" The tension drained out of Grace. "Oh, come on, Minny, you have to do better than that if you want to scare me."

Something her cousin used to take delight in when she'd been a teenager and in charge of Grace and Corbett.

"I'm not trying to scare you."

A chill ran through Grace, but she chased it away. Minny had always used her psychic abilities to make herself seem more mysterious and all-knowing.

"I really do need to get ready for my shoot," Grace said, all business now.

Tension made it impossible to get her lipstick on just right—Minny wasn't taking the hint and leaving!

"Uh-uh, Grace. You haven't told me about the psychic incident yet. Did you touch this Declan?"

"What does it matter?" Grace asked, even as what she'd seen flitted through her mind. "I don't have the ability anymore. I don't want to be psychic."

"You don't have any say in the matter. The sooner you come to terms with that, the better. So what was it? A real live look into the future? Or were you simply reading what was on his mind?"

She hadn't really thought about it before. Maybe Declan had been the one on the hormonal overload and she'd merely been picking that up. Not that the possibility made her feel any better. Psychic was psychic and she didn't want any part of the supposed gift. Or maybe her imagination had simply been engaged. Declan was someone she'd hired to work for her, and that was that.

"You encouraged me to use my touch before, Minny, and look where it got me," Grace reminded her. "Humiliated in front of my classmates."

The last time she'd read anyone's thoughts, she'd been fifteen. Years of predictions had made her a pariah amongst her peers because kids didn't like anyone who was different. That last time, she'd made such a muddle interpreting what she'd seen that she'd sworn never to succumb to that particular temptation again. Her decision to abstain from mind-reading had relieved her family—all but Cousin Minny, of course. Minny understood Grace's gift because she'd been the only other person in the family who'd had the touch since their grandmama had passed.

"It takes maturity and practice to get things right," Minny said. "It's not like listening to a radio. Lots of times you have to untangle what you hear to make sense of it." Minny leaned over and gave her a hug and a kiss on the cheek. "Try to chill, would you? And let me know when you're ready to expand your mind again."

Which would be never.

Still, Grace hugged Minny in return. She loved her cousin even if she didn't want to be like her.

"Remember what I said about the bustier," Minny reminded her. "Bad vibes."

"I'll remember."

But Grace meant to wear it anyway. It was her job.

After putting on the bustier, she stood in front of the mirror and aligned it on her body.

The garment really was sexy, pushing her full breasts up over the delicate material so that her flesh looked ready to spill out of the top. As she adjusted the shallow lacy cups, she couldn't help but wonder how Declan would react if he saw her wearing this.

Grace struck a sultry pose as she would in front of the camera and gave her imagination free rein.

Suddenly it came to her again—that image she'd gotten when she'd taken Declan's hand. Unable to help herself, she cupped her breasts as he might do. Her neck arched and her breathing changed and her breasts swelled until her nipples peaked over the top of the lace.

She licked her lips and closed her eyes for a moment and indulged herself in a moment of fantasy about a sexy man.

Suddenly, she got the weirdest sensation, almost feeling as if Declan were watching her. Her eyes whipped open and she stared at herself in the mirror.

No, not Declan…

Someone else.

Having the same feeling she'd had several times in the past weeks, she tugged the bustier in place and gave the room a paranoid once-over, expecting to see a peephole in the wall somewhere. Nothing. Of course not. Her imagination was simply running wild.

Thank you, Minny, she thought as she slipped into a robe.

Shaking off the creepy feeling only with difficulty, Grace quickly finished getting ready for the shoot, all the while wondering what Declan might have found out.

"Is Ms. Broussard expectin' you?" the hefty woman in the gray uniform asked.

"No, actually not…" Declan quickly looked at the uniform's pocket where the woman's name was scrolled. "Eula. But I have business with Ms. Broussard."

The guard narrowed her gaze at Declan before nodding. "All right, go on in. But if Ms. Broussard ain't pleased to see you, you'll answer to me."

"Absolutely," Declan said, as he headed for the door with the Gotcha! sign.

Declan entered the photography studio office and noted the unoccupied desk set in the middle of an empty and none-too-lovingly decorated room. The place was at best functional, though no receptionist guarded the gates to the inner sanctum.

Music drifted from an open doorway to the right. Declan stepped inside the studio, following the strains of a sexy tune—a woman with a low, throbbing voice warbling in French. He stood back in the dark.

Before him, in a pool of hazy lavender light, lying

across a chaise lounge, Grace Broussard made love to the camera in time to the sensual music. And as she did, another woman with spiked, magenta-streaked brown hair, wearing short-shorts and a tube top, photographed her. This was Max? For a moment, Declan watched her work. Max Babin was a total professional and he got no bad vibes from her, so he turned back to the woman she was photographing.

Dressed in a cream-colored bustier, lace cheeky panties, thigh-high stockings and sling-back sandals, Grace was every man's dream. And what she did with her body as the camera whirled softly! Max barely had to encourage her to adopt poses that made Declan physically uncomfortable.

This was work, he reminded himself. Not play.

On her knees, she stretched like a cat….

She turned on her side and lifted one leg in a seemingly impossible pose….

Then she was on her back, both legs drawn over the top of the chaise, her upper body dangling, head down….

The very atmosphere was charged with Grace's sexuality, and Declan was a mere man, one who'd been without female companionship for too long. He wondered how he was going to work for Grace without getting himself in a knot around her.

"That should do it," Max said none-too-soon.

"Good. I'm exhausted."

Grace stood and walked out of the pool of light where she slipped into a silky robe. Declan cleared his throat to make his presence known.

The photographer immediately whipped around, her eyes squinting into the dark. "Who's there?"

"Declan McKenna," he said, stepping into the light. "I'm a friend of Grace's."

Grace's eyes went wide. "Uh, Declan…" Her voice throbbed, sounding thick and undeniably sexy. "Let's go to my dressing room."

"Yes, let's," he said agreeably.

When they entered the cramped room, which was little bigger than a closet, she asked, "What brings you here, Declan? The fingerprints? Did you get the results back already?"

"On the weekend? No such luck. I simply thought it would be a good idea for me to see where you work. Where you live."

"You want to come home with me?"

"Don't you want me to make sure your place is safe? If you really do have a stalker—"

"If? You don't believe me, after all. For your information, I'm pretty sure someone was following me last night after I left your office."

"What happened?"

"I'm fine, aren't I? Part of me thinks I was imagining things."

"Even so, the possibility gives me more reason to

check out your place—to make sure that if someone is doing more than just sending you notes, he can't get at you."

"Fine. You can come home with me and check things out, then. But I would appreciate your waiting in the outer office while I change."

"No problem."

While he would rather remain right where he was, Declan knew that would lead to nothing but trouble.

Though he hadn't yet gotten a report on the fingerprints, he'd called Ian to see if his cousin knew anything about their client. Declan hadn't been in New Orleans long enough to get more than the feel of the place, but Ian had lived here all his life. Indeed, Ian had known that Grace Broussard was a trust-fund baby and something of a free spirit in a political, driven family.

Obviously, she'd found her niche, Declan thought, and a perfect one for her, at that.

And now someone was threatening to use it against her.

Not on his watch.

GRACE'S NERVES WERE already on edge. She'd been occupied for every moment since she'd had that bizarre feeling in her dressing room that morning, but once she stopped working, she couldn't forget about it. She found herself changing in the powder room, as if she were safe in the smaller space.

But safe from what?

The scariest thing she had to face was touching Declan again. The mere thought of which sent a shiver down her spine, all the way to her toes.

So a few minutes later, as they walked along Decatur and its shops filled with tourist trinkets and other souvenirs of New Orleans, Grace made certain she kept a safe distance between them.

"Do you always work on Saturdays?" Declan asked.

"No. We just had to finish up shooting the new designs for a series of ads Raphael intends to run."

"Very provocative."

She slashed him a look. "You don't approve?"

"I was simply making an observation," Declan said, his demeanor professional. He moved his gaze constantly over the crowd as if searching it for a potential stalker. "So do people recognize you when you walk down the street?"

"So far people haven't actually come up to me and told me so."

"Just followed you."

"Which would be scarier," she said.

"What happens when Raphael Duhon goes really big? Will you follow him to New York? Paris?"

"I never thought that far ahead. I like things as

they are now. New Orleans is my home. I have a great job and I'm close to Mama and my brother, Corbett." Just considering losing all that made Grace uneasy. She was happy now. "I can't see wanting any of that to change."

"You can't control fate."

Grace didn't miss the serious note in Declan's tone. She wondered what had happened to him to make him such a cynic.

As they walked through the French Quarter, her native city called to her, stirring her blood. Music and the seductive voices of entrepreneurs floated on the air along with the smell of Cajun and Creole cooking. New Orleans was a city of the senses and Grace was in love with her hometown, grateful its heart had survived disaster. It had taken years, but finally it was coming back from Hurricane Katrina.

They walked up past Esplanade and then away from the river. Grace lived in an old apartment complex in Faubourg Marigny, a neighborhood bordering the French Quarter. Her third-floor apartment had a balcony with black wrought-iron railings that wrapped around the corner from living room to bedroom.

"Not what you would call a secure building," Declan said when they found the downstairs door unlocked.

"Some people think they're bulletproof," she

muttered, releasing the latch so not just anyone could get in.

"That door needs a dead bolt."

Grace knew he was correct, but she didn't know what it would take to convince her landlord. They headed for the third floor. Her newspaper lay outside her apartment door. When she picked it up, she saw what it had been hiding.

"What's this?" she muttered, stooping again to pick up a large brown envelope.

Her name and nothing else was typed on the label stuck on the front. No postage. Someone had hand-delivered it—an easy task since someone had left the downstairs door unlocked. Her pulse thudded. Or maybe whoever had left it had picked the lock and that's why the door was open.

"Something wrong?"

"I don't know." Grace stared at the envelope as if she could guess its contents—something she wasn't going to like.

"Let's get inside."

She was barely through the door when she moved around the counter in the kitchen area to keep distance between her and Declan. Wanting to see what was inside the envelope before he did, she ripped it open, then tilted it to spill the contents into her hand. A glossy photograph of her.

Shocked, Grace went still and wide-eyed.

The woman in the photograph was and was not her. She managed to appear seductive in the ads modeling Raphael's designs, but this woman was wanton.

Her eyes were closed, her head thrown back, her breasts half-spilled out of the bustier. The facial expression got to Grace, tied her stomach in a knot. This woman looked like she was in the throes of passion. Her face left nothing to the imagination.

She'd been warned—*I CAN EXPOSE YOU*—and now the threat was a reality.

"Oh, my God," she whispered, wondering how the photo had been taken without her knowledge.

She'd done a lot of crazy things, but basically her march to freedom from the Broussards had been innocent stuff. Posing for pornography hadn't been anything she'd ever contemplated.

She looked in the envelope and found a note still clinging to the side.

THERE ARE MORE WHERE THIS CAME FROM. HOW MUCH IS THE DISK WORTH TO YOUR FAMILY? CHECK YOUR E-MAIL AT MIDNIGHT TONIGHT FOR INSTRUCTIONS.

Chapter Three

Grace sounded appalled when she said, "This looks like I posed for an adult magazine!"

Her horror washed over Declan and he was hard pressed not to step forward and take her in his arms to bring her down. "I take it you didn't pose for whatever is there."

"Of course not. This was taken in the dressing room this morning when I was getting ready for the shoot. What if it gets out? It could ruin Mama's chances at the judgeship. And Corbett could lose the upcoming election. There must have been a hidden camera… Who could have done this? Why does someone want to blackmail me?"

"Can I see?" Declan asked, holding out a hand.

She flipped the photograph to her breast. "No!"

"How am I supposed to help you if I don't know what I'm dealing with?"

"Use your imagination."

He doubted anything she'd done in front of a camera could be as racy as where his mind took him. "It's probably not as bad as you think."

"It's worse."

Declan fell silent. He couldn't force her to show him the photograph. Her escalating emotions bombarded him—fear, hurt, panic—and he stared at her hard enough to make her squirm visibly.

"All right." She set everything down on the counter between them. "Go ahead. Look."

The moment she gave him permission, Grace turned her back on him as if she didn't want to see his reaction. Her tension was palpable and quickly spread to him.

Declan flipped the photograph over. She was right—it was a lot worse than he'd thought. And better. He couldn't help his appreciation as his imagination put the woman in the photograph right into his bed.

Reading the note, he knew he needed to play it cool, to hide what he was really feeling. "Blackmail," he murmured. "This is serious, Grace. Time to take this to the authorities."

"Are you out of your mind? I go to the police and those photos become public knowledge. I can't do that to Mama and Corbett—their careers will be destroyed."

But he suspected a photo like this would probably

give her career a boost. Even so, Declan figured she had to be upset at the violation of her own privacy.

"Come on, sit." He led her into the living area and waited until she threw herself into a chair. "Perhaps the police could be persuaded to keep the case low-key."

Grace forced a laugh. "I don't want anyone seeing me like this. Maybe Raphael can help us catch the creep."

"*If* this Raphael is on the up-and-up." He paused a minute before asking, "How do you know he's not the one who put the camera in your dressing room?"

"No, not Raphael. That doesn't make any sense. He wouldn't want to ruin the connection I have with the public."

"Or he could think a little scandal will up sales."

"No," she said again, her chest tightening. "How will I get out of this? What do you propose I do now?" she asked Declan. "Other than going to the police."

"You say Raphael and Max are the only ones with access to the photography studio on a regular basis?"

"Right. Raphael occupies the whole third floor for both Voodoo offices and his living quarters."

Declan took the chair opposite her. "Offices… Do a lot of people work for him?"

"He has a personal assistant, a design assistant, a cutter and sewer to execute the early incarnations of his designs, a saleswoman and a receptionist."

"Lots of possible suspects."

"I guess. He has an office at another location. That's where the marketing and financial people are located. He also owns two other buildings in the French Quarter and a few in the Commercial District. One of those didn't fare too well when Hurricane Katrina hit. I understand there was a problem with the insurance. As far as I know, he still doesn't have it ready for rental."

"Not in all this time?" Declan mused. "Sounds like Raphael might have some money troubles."

"Well, he's put a lot into Voodoo, which is his real love," Grace said. "He's been working for other people for years and finally got his own business off the ground. You don't really believe a man suddenly shooting to the top of his profession would involve himself in blackmail, do you?"

Thinking blackmail money might be just the thing to get that commercial building up and running— not to mention Voodoo, possibly the reason Raphael gave a trust-fund baby work—Declan said, "Hard to say what anyone would do where money is involved. I'll be checking on his other properties, see what's going on. Who else works in your building?"

"There are a couple other businesses, but I don't know any of those people—I can't imagine they even know I'm around. As to Max," Grace went on evenly, "she has a part-time photography assistant who sets up the set. She works when needed and that's it. Usually Max has a full-time employee who does some of everything—reception, billing, secretarial—but she let Eva go and hasn't talked about replacing her. I don't think it was Eva's work. I suspect Max couldn't afford to keep her."

Making the photographer another suspect, Declan thought. "I'm going to need a list of everyone who works in the building so I can run security checks on them."

"Okay, I can put that together for you."

"Good. If you add the building employees, that offers more variables to the situation. Lots of people who have access to the studio and therefore the dressing room."

"I wouldn't know where to start."

"How about we start by finding the camera—assuming it's still in place. If we're lucky we can track it back to its source."

Grace shuddered. "The studio isn't open."

"Even better."

"You want to break in?"

"The security guard—will it be the one who was on duty earlier?"

"Eula? I'm not sure."

"Well, hope she is. She seemed to like you."

"She's always been friendly to me."

"Then chances are you can talk our way back into the place."

On the way back to the studio, Declan couldn't erase the photograph in his mind. He tried—really—but his libido was stronger than his will, at least in this case. He kept seeing Grace in undergarments that begged to be removed.

So when he opened the door of the taxi he'd hailed for her and she sort of ducked so as not to touch him as she slid inside, he was a bit relieved. But when he noticed that Grace was practically huddling against the opposite door leaving two feet of space between them, Declan tried not to take offense.

"So what's this event we're going to later?" he asked, thinking talking would relax her.

"It's a bipartisan fund-raiser for the local schools. Mama was on the committee that put it together."

"It doesn't sound like your kind of scene."

"It isn't. But I support my family. And the kids. The schools still don't have everything they need. If I can do something to make it happen, you bet I will."

The fervor in her voice got to Declan. So Grace was more than a pretty face.

The taxi stopped at the studio. While Declan paid, Grace let herself out. She went inside and raced up the steps to the second floor. Sure enough, Eula was still at the security desk.

"Miss Grace, what you doin' back here?" she asked. "Don't tell me Ms. Babin is makin' you work tonight."

"Oh, no. I'm not working. I'm going to a party tonight. That's the problem—I can't find my invitation. I must have left it in the dressing room."

"You need an invitation to get in?"

"It's sort of an invitation-receipt for the school fund-raiser. My mother is on the committee and wouldn't be happy if I didn't show up."

"Your mama's a smart lady," Eula said to her while eyeing Declan with suspicion. "I hear she's gonna be a judge."

"She's hoping. At any rate, I was showing the invitation to my cousin and I guess I never put it back in my bag. Can you let me in, Eula?"

"Sure, no problem." The security guard stepped out from behind her desk. "Follow me." But when Declan started off, as well, Eula gave him another piercing look. "Where do you think you're goin'?"

Seeing that Eula's bristles were up, Declan winked at her. "I can't let this woman out of my sight. I'm sure you know how that is."

But Eula didn't relax until Declan slipped an arm around Grace's waist. Then it was Grace who became instantly uptight. He felt the tension the moment he touched her. Still, she forced a convincing smile.

"Declan's helping me will make the search go faster, Eula," she choked out.

"Okay, okay," Eula muttered, leading the way to the Gotcha! entrance.

Declan took a quick look at Grace, who wiggled out from the protection of his arm. Tension was evident in her beautiful features.

Just from his touching her?

Stopping in front of the photography studio door, Eula sorted through keys on a heavy ring until she found the right one. Seconds later, the door stood open.

"Okay, there you go now."

Grace gave the other woman a warm smile. "Thank you, Eula."

Declan let Grace take the lead inside, but he made sure to close the door behind them.

Declan reached past her and turned the doorknob. "Ladies first."

When he pulled back, he brushed her in the process. She practically jumped away from him. For a second, her gaze went blank, as though she were somewhere else. Declan was hit by a sense of panic that didn't make any sense. Then Grace quickly gathered herself and went inside the dressing room. She flicked on the light, then slowly turned, her gaze furtively darting around the room.

"I don't see anything."

"Slow down. Think about the angle from which

the photograph was taken. The camera had to be in front of you. So which way were you facing?"

"The mirror."

"The camera wasn't straight on—"

"It was up a little," she finished for him.

They both looked up, over the mirror.

Declan's gaze settled on the mirror frame itself—about four inches wide with a shiny black finish. Tall enough to reach over, he ran his fingers along the edge of the mirror.

"Got it," he muttered, "and it's Wi-Fi." He ran his fingers over the front of the frame, then tapped the spot where a small chunk of wood had been drilled out. "The lens such as it is lines up right here."

"I can't see anything."

"The shiny black paint presents you with an optical illusion, but there is a peephole. If you look closely, you can see it."

Grace moved closer so that she was almost touching him. "There it is. Wireless, huh? It'll make it easier to pull out."

"We don't want to do that. If all else fails, we might be able to trap whoever did this with his own camera."

"In the meantime, there's an unwanted set of eyes in the dressing room."

"So don't dress in front of the mirror." What he was really thinking was that she shouldn't play out her fantasies except in the privacy of her own home, but he didn't think she would appreciate the advice. She'd already learned the hard way. "Just in case, let me check the room over. And the powder room."

"All right," Grace conceded, aiming a resentful glare at the hiding place as she sank into a chair.

Declan felt her eyes on him as he searched every nook and cranny. And her emotions. They were in a whirl. Anger mixed with hurt. He realized she couldn't conceive of anyone betraying her like this. He wanted to put his arms around her and tell her that he would catch the creep and stop the blackmail and everything would be all right. Only he wasn't sure it would be that easy. And, from her attitude toward him, she apparently didn't want him to touch her.

He could only speculate on the reason—her emotions told him what she was feeling, but they didn't explain why.

"The room seems to be clear other than the camera we found," Declan said. "How much time do you think we have before Eula comes looking for us?"

"I don't know. Maybe a bit. She's pretty relaxed. Usually."

"Then let's take advantage of every moment and check out Max's office."

Leading the way out the door, she asked, "What do you expect to find there?"

"A Wi-Fi camera can send a signal to a compatible printer or computer."

"I'm not what you would call a techie."

"Don't worry, our firm can high tech along with the best of them. My cousin Ian makes sure we keep up with the latest gadgets."

"You think Max is the one, don't you?"

"The people here are the most logical suspects. Cameras are Max's thing, after all, and this is her business."

"Seems too easy to me," she said. "She'd know that I would figure it out and press charges."

"But if she's getting big bucks from someone for doing this, she could think it's worth the risk. You have to know that whoever did this is probably counting on the fact that you love your family too much to see their careers destroyed."

A quick tour of Max's office did show that both her printer and her desktop computer had a wireless card. But if there was a file with the explicit photos of Grace stored on the system, Declan couldn't identify it. He enjoyed checking out the shots he did find—Grace posing for Voodoo ads. She didn't need to be exposing herself to have him where it hurt. His imagination set in motion once more, he found it difficult to concentrate, so he shut down the computer and continued on a physical search of the office.

When they reached for the same file drawer, their hands touched. Declan froze. He didn't know how much temptation he could take. Grace got that weird expression again. Then she blinked and came back and Declan was more tempted than ever to kiss her....

"Hey, Miss Grace, where are you?"

They scrambled away from each other as Eula strode into the office. Luckily the computer was down and no drawers were open so the whole thing looked pretty innocent.

"What you doin' in here?"

"The invitation," she said breathlessly, pulling something from her trouser pocket and waving it at the guard. "Look, I just found it."

"Good for you. Bergeron wants to get in here and clean and I told him to wait a minute so he didn't disturb you."

"Tell him the place is his," Grace said. "And thank you so much. Now I won't have to make my excuses to Mama."

"She might put you in jail, eh?" Eula said with a laugh as they all left Max Babin's office.

"Mama might consider it a crime if I didn't make it to the fund-raiser, but she might have a hard time putting me behind bars simply for being a no-show."

"You never know who she might decide to prosecute," Eula said.

When they stepped out of the studio, Declan saw a man in khakis leaning on a cleaning cart. He didn't look as anxious to get started as the security guard suggested.

"Hey, Bergeron, we're out of your way," Grace called cheerfully.

Giving her a sour look, Bergeron merely grunted in return and shoved his cart through the door.

Sensing a wave of something dark, something he couldn't quite define, Declan murmured, "Friendly, huh?"

"He's new. He started working here about a month ago. He's always like that with everyone." Grace practically flew down the stairs.

Declan had to work to keep up with her.

"Good thinking," he said. "Bringing the invitation with you."

"What invitation? This is a dry-cleaning receipt I forgot to take out of my pocket."

Declan would laugh, but nothing about this situation was funny. Flagging down a taxi to take them back to Grace's place, Declan knew that, despite her sophisticated looks, Grace Broussard was an innocent swimming with sharks.

He didn't need to see outward signs to know what a person was made of. His empathic ability let him read her easily—her warmheartedness, her inner fragility, her uncertainty when it came to herself. Grace was a woman who didn't deserve to have anything bad happen to her.

Declan was determined that nothing would.

Chapter Four

Despite her best intentions, Grace hadn't been able to avoid touching Declan a few times. And when she'd touched him, she hadn't been able to avoid seeing them together intimately.

On edge as she dragged herself up the stairs to her apartment, she said, "Well, that certainly was a waste of time and effort."

"Not a waste. We know where the camera is now."

"I would rather have ripped it out and ground it under my heel."

"Destroy evidence?"

"Evidence for what?"

"To make an arrest."

Grace shook her head and unlocked her door. "Who said I was having anyone arrested?"

"This is blackmail! Don't you want to see justice done?"

"I'm thinking in terms of a bonfire." Entering, she

threw her keys on a nearby table. "Camera. All copies of the photographs. The rat responsible."

"Well, yeah, burning him at the stake might be rewarding, but it's also illegal."

"Afraid I might take the law into my own hands?" Declan closed the door, asking, "You're serious about not wanting to prosecute anyone?"

"Look, I don't ever want my family to know about this fiasco. I certainly don't want it to get out, which it would if I pressed charges."

"You didn't pose for those photographs. And it's not like you're having sex with anyone in them."

"Mama is already disapproving of my work. This would give her a great I-told-you-so moment." She felt him stop behind her so close she imagined his breath ruffling her hair.

"Grace, I can't believe you would let your mother's disapproval stop you from doing the right thing."

"Right thing?" She whirled to face him—too close for comfort, but she stood her ground. "According to Mama, if I wanted to do the right thing, I would have gotten a degree and started a professional career years ago. Preferably in politics. If I wanted to do the right thing, I would have chosen someone suitable to marry. Old money, social register. If I wanted to do the right thing, I wouldn't embarrass her on a weekly basis because the ads I pose for make the men of New Orleans desire me."

"You wouldn't have to pose for ads to be desired."

"This isn't the time for jokes, Declan."

His expression taut, he murmured, "Who's joking?"

"If we could figure out who put that camera in the dressing room and have him arrested, you can bet the media will have the story within hours if not sooner. I would be lucky if that photograph didn't make the front page of the *Times-Picayune*. It would get around. Mama could kiss the bench goodbye. Corbett wouldn't be able to run for dog-catcher. And I wouldn't be able to show my face in polite society ever again."

"I got the idea you didn't care for polite society."

"*I'm* not a snob, Declan. I just wish other people weren't. But I don't want to be humiliated again."

"Again? When was the first time?"

Remembering the way her gift had misled her—the way she'd been laughed at had dogged her footsteps through the years—Grace clenched her jaw. No way was she going to tell Declan about the humiliating incident. No way would she give him the chance to laugh at her, too.

"Hey," he said softly, stepping closer. "I didn't mean to upset you."

"It's not you. It just comes with the territory."

"What territory?"

"Being me" was all she would admit to. "It's almost time to put on my game face." When he appeared confused, she clarified. "The fund-raiser tonight? I'm going to have to make my appearance and then like Cinderella, do a disappearing act so I can be in front of a computer screen at midnight."

"Is that going to be doable?"

"That's where you come in—make it happen."

"So what time should I pick you up?"

"I was thinking about that." Grabbing a notepad and pen, she scribbled down the information he needed. "Meet me there about nine."

"You don't want to be seen with me?"

"Once you're there I do. Make it seem like we ran into each other. And figure out a cover story for what you do. If the blackmailer is at the party, I don't want to give him a heads-up that I hired a P.I."

"You're the boss."

Declan left to get ready for the party, and Grace had to admit she was interested in him more than she wanted to be. Certain that he was interested in return, she wondered for how long. Experience told her that eventually Declan McKenna would be the same as the other men she knew and would expect her to change.

And if he found out about her gift of touch…

Declan was a wild card. Why had he resurrected her latent psychic ability? No matter that she kept trying to talk herself out of the fact, there it was. Either she was projecting into their future or she was reading what was on his mind. Whichever didn't really matter. She didn't trust the visions. She didn't trust Declan, not personally.

Stopping in front of a table with gilt edging, she looked at the photos on display. The one of her with Mama and Daddy and Corbett had been taken when she was eight. Against the almost Gothic-looking dark clothing the entire family wore, she posed stiffly in bright pink shoes that Cousin Minny had bought for her at the French Market. Grace remembered wearing only those shoes for months no matter what threat Mama made. A small defiance.

The other photo was of her in her first Voodoo ad, looking comfortably sensual and happy, as if she'd finally found herself—which she had. She was more than a Broussard, Grace thought. She *was* Voodoo Woman. Wearing these clothes, posing for the camera, she could be and do anything she wanted. Donning Raphael's designs were magic—they transformed her.

Grace never had felt like she fit in with her immediate family. While Daddy had had something of a relaxed attitude, he was gone now. And Mama was Mama. Old New Orleans blue blood, social register. Corbett wasn't much better. Her brother might do what he wanted, but in secret, careful of appearances. Only once had he gotten careless. Reporter Naomi Larkin had proven to have a reputation for sleeping with men to get a juicy story, and Corbett had been one of her marks.

Mama never let Corbett forget about Naomi. Grace wasn't about to let Mama get any ammunition on *her,* not if she could help it.

Always knowing she stuck out like a sore thumb as had her pink shoes in the early photo, Grace had searched for someplace, something that would define her. Raphael had given her that chance when he'd hired her to be the spokeswoman for his company and she'd started wearing his clothes almost exclusively. She'd come to terms with a new and pleasing image of herself.

And then someone had gone and destroyed that comfort zone by hiding a camera in the dressing room.

Thinking about the photograph taken without permission depressed her. In some strange way, Grace felt it was a judgment against her personal choices. Something essential to her mental well-being— something she'd gained only in the past year—had been stolen from her.

The thing was, she knew how to hide what she was really feeling. She'd learned from the best. No matter the situation, she could breathe and smile and pretend whatever someone did to her didn't matter. She would project the image necessary for the evening as well as any other woman present.

Determined to forget about Declan and the blackmail scheme for the moment and put her mind to the cause of the evening, Grace stepped into the shower.

DECLAN DECIDED to stop by the office before heading home and was surprised to find his cousin Ian had returned from his field trip and was sitting at the receptionist's desk at the computer. Ian was McKenna through and through—tall and broad-shouldered, with the black Irish good looks of all the men in their family. The one thing to set him apart was the color of his eyes.

Ian had forever taken a bashing over their muddy-violet hue, never as evident as when he looked up at Declan. "I finished earlier than expected."

"Did you get what you needed?" Declan asked him.

"More than enough to convince Mrs. Randolph that her husband is not only having an affair, but also that he's giving away marital monies. He bought the blonde an estate in the Lake Charles area worth upwards of a million dollars."

"Does it ever bother you? Breaking up marriages?"

"I would say hold Mr. Randolph responsible for that, not me. I'm just reporting the truth of the matter. You need to loosen up, Declan. What private investigators do is a lot less structured than police work."

"And usually less rewarding."

Declan had worked for several years as a detective in the Criminal Investigation Division in Santa

Fe. He wished he could say being a private investigator was equally fulfilling, but more often than not, his cases in the past six months since they'd opened their own investigation agency had been simple, bordering on boring. So far, Declan had avoided marriage disputes—Ian didn't mind them—but he figured it was only a matter of time before his number came up.

"The thought of getting in the middle of someone else's love life doesn't appeal to me," Declan said.

"You'll get used to it."

"No one could ever accuse you of being a romantic."

Ian snorted. "You're romantic enough for the both of us. Turning in your resignation on a job that was your life and leaving town all because of a supposed curse by some jealous witch of a woman." He shook his head.

"Hey, it affects you, too, Ian."

"If I believed in curses."

"How can you not when you've seen the things that have happened to other McKennas who were descendants of Donal?" Declan asked. "Or what happened to my mother? Nothing like a scorned witch good at casting spells."

Should Donal McKenna's descendants find love and act on their feelings, they would put their loved ones in mortal danger. McKenna loves had died from illness, accident and even murder—and they'd all been young. Considering their McKenna relatives all had abilities that regular people didn't, how could Ian shut his mind to the possibility that Sheelin O'Keefe had indeed cast a powerful hex on them all?

"As a private investigator, I've seen all kinds of terrible things happen in relationships," Ian said. "Maybe we're all doomed to heartache and unhappiness and we just aren't aware of it until it happens to us."

"Not everyone loses the love of their life to death."

His mother had died from a mysterious fall before Declan was even born—he'd been taken surgically from her lifeless body. His survival had been a miracle. His father had remarried and Declan had several half siblings, but that relationship had been built on respect, not on romantic love. As an empath, Declan was as aware of that as he was of his father's limited love for him. Padraig McKenna blamed him for the loss of the love of his life—not that he ever said so. But from the time he was a boy, Declan had sensed it, had sensed the difference in what Da felt for him compared to the others. It was something he had to live with, something he would never pass down to a child of his own.

"Now you're just being dramatic," Ian said. "There are McKennas very happily married."

"But not without overcoming danger…and some of them aren't married to their true loves," Declan countered, wondering if Grace had ever found hers and had her heart broken. Thinking of the woman, he said, "Back to the new case I took on last night. I'm going to a charity event tonight where I'll meet with Grace Broussard."

"Lucky man."

"It's business, Ian."

"She *is* single."

"And a client." Though a very beautiful, very desirable, very vulnerable woman.

"Which means you need to act in her best interests…whatever that entails." Ian winked.

Sensing a surge of unadulterated lust wash over him from his cousin, Declan said, "Don't get any ideas."

"I appreciate the package, but she's not my type. I want a woman with drive and big appetites for everything."

Despite himself, Declan asked, "How do you know Grace doesn't qualify?"

"I might not know Grace Broussard personally, but I know *of* her. At least enough to read her."

Having grown up in New Orleans, having worked for a major private investigations firm before they started their own, his cousin had the pulse of the rich and famous, knew where the bodies were buried, so to speak.

"There's more to her than you give her credit for," Declan said.

Ian shrugged. "Grace Broussard has gone through life without goals. She went from school to school, job to job, never earning a degree, never settling down to a career, never developing a long-lasting relationship with a man."

"Until Voodoo."

"If you call that a career."

"What would *you* call it?"

"A distraction. It won't last, Declan. Nothing with Ms. Broussard ever does."

"I didn't get that from her."

"Using your abilities to read her, are you?"

"You have an argument against my using another tool to help my client?"

"If that's your story…"

"It's not a story. Grace Broussard came to me for help. She thought it was an annoyance—a stalker—but there's more to it. Someone is trying to blackmail her."

"That's a new turn. For doing what?"

"For doing her job."

"You mean photographs?"

"Someone installed a hidden camera in her dressing room."

Ian whistled. "What does the blackmailer want?"

"Don't know yet. The demand will be e-mailed at midnight. I might need some of your expertise to track the e-mail back to the sender."

"No problem. Let me know what you need."

"I will. In the meantime, I'd better get out of here and change."

Checking his watch, Declan realized he had to hurry. Luckily his apartment was a quick walk from the office. Once inside, he was showered and dressed in ten minutes. And in another five, he was on his way to the hotel.

Declan couldn't help but mull over what he'd learned from his cousin about Grace. A woman who didn't get herself involved in long-term relationships. Perfect. She might be a client now, but that would change when he solved the case. He was already looking forward to the possibilities.

CARS AND TAXIS LINED UP outside the Hotel Monteleone. Declan looked for Grace as he went inside. No luck there, either. Not that she couldn't be in the ballroom. It was already swarming with guests.

Declan wandered through the crowd, his intent not only to find her, but also to read the guests, as well. Empathic impressions weren't as accurate an ability as telepathy, for example, but taking the pulse of the room had always served him well, perhaps the reason he'd had such a good arrest and conviction record as a cop.

As he walked through the crowd, Declan opened himself to the people around him who didn't even notice he was there. Most people were into themselves, projecting a particular face to the room—success, interest, openness—while casting out vibes at odds with those facades.

He sensed uncertainty…contempt…awe…remorse.

Unfortunately he could only take the crowd's pulse. It would demand a face-to-face to get a clearer picture of how any particular emotion played out in a given situation.

Suddenly the tenor of the room changed, lust being the overriding emotion sizzling off the men around him. Declan turned, his gaze fixed on the entrance where he caught a glimpse of a gown that shimmered and glowed as brightly as the crystal chandeliers overhead.

Dressed in a backless tight column of red sequins, Grace Broussard entered the ballroom alone. She looked poised…relaxed…in charge.

All an illusion.

Declan wasn't close enough to read her as accurately as he might like, but even at a distance, he sensed her anxiety and an underlying fear that, under the circumstances, was totally understandable.

Chapter Five

Grace felt rather than saw heads turn when she entered the hotel ballroom. She was posing, pretending—not that she was someone else, but that she was as confident as she appeared. Inside, she was a trembling, pitiful mess. She probably should have had Declan escort her here.

Gazing around the room for the private investigator, she couldn't miss the attention she was getting. For once she wished she could leave again, so she could go find a place to hide where she didn't have to think about suggestive photographs and someone's evil intent.

Was the blackmailer in the room now?

Would she be able to tell if she saw him?

How would she know when she couldn't even look anyone in the eyes?

Spotting Raphael was a relief. As usual, her employer was dressed in black. And as usual, he wore ruby studs in his ears and a gold snake with ruby eyes on the middle finger of his right hand. His slicked, long, black hair accentuated chiseled features and slightly slanted brown eyes.

Raphael gave her a high sign before turning back to his young male companion.

Then she spotted Corbett and made straight for her brother. As usual, his tux was perfectly tailored and not a strand of his golden-brown hair was out of place. His eyebrows shot up and his hazel eyes widened appreciatively.

"Grace, won't *you* kick up Mama's ulcer tonight."

"If she actually had an ulcer, this dress might do it," she agreed. "So, are you here alone?"

"I am. Although I have my eye on an interesting woman new to the political game in this town. What about you?"

Thinking of Declan again, Grace felt her pulse rush, but she said, "Alone for the moment, as well."

"Well, this little event might be interesting, after all."

"I'm hoping." Grace tried to keep her tone casual so she wouldn't warn Corbett something was wrong. "Anyone I should know to be careful around? Someone with a grudge against you or Mama?"

"Grudge? Not exactly. But there is Larry Laroche. He'll be running against me for my seat on the city council."

"Sounds as if you have reason to not like the man."

"I don't have proof of anything of course, but rumor has it he'll do anything to win."

"Anything?" Grace's interest picked up. *Like hiring someone to take questionable photos of his opponent's sister?*

"He smeared his last opponent, Tommy Ryan, the other candidate in his own party. His colleagues weren't too happy with him, but he just shrugged off the censure."

"Smeared Ryan how?"

"Sent a reporter to the bordello where Ryan was…well, occupied."

"A sex scandal? How did I miss it?"

"Because it never hit the media. Tommy bought off the reporter. But word got around, courtesy of Laroche, and the next thing you know, Tommy is no longer in the running. He concedes and the victory goes to Laroche."

"And you're sure this information is accurate?"

"As sure as I can be of my sources. So don't go getting yourself into some big scandal before the election or Laroche will use it against me."

Grace swallowed hard. Corbett was dead serious. Knowing his temper, she hoped she could keep word of those photographs from getting to him forever.

"I'll try to contain myself for your sake."

Corbett grinned at her. "Good, and if you have

the chance, chat up Jill Westerfield. See what you can find out about her."

"Is that the woman new to the game?"

"One and the same."

Grace followed her brother's gaze to a woman who was tall, curvaceous and wore her blond hair short, scraped back from her face. Something about the blonde ticked at Grace, but she couldn't place her. A simple black sheath and horn-rimmed glasses did little to distract from Jill Westerfield's attractiveness. The blonde stopped next to Laroche and put a possessive hand on his shoulder. The politician smiled at her and immediately wrapped an arm around her waist.

"Um…looks like she has a date for the evening. With a married man."

"I can overlook that," Corbett said, a predatory gleam in his eyes.

Wondering where Laroche's wife might be, Grace couldn't fathom why her brother was interested in a woman who would go after the sleazy politician. "Nothing like picking someone totally inappropriate."

"Perhaps I'll get her to cross the line, come over to my way of thinking."

It had been years since her brother had seemed so focused on a woman—Naomi had been pre-Katrina—and Grace didn't want to discourage him. For years he'd had "safe" dates, none of whom had ever put that particular gleam in his eyes, so she kept her thoughts to herself. Maybe she was just misreading the relationship between the Westerfield woman and Laroche.

"What about Mama?" she asked. "Does she have to be careful of someone, too?"

Corbett gave her his you-should-know-better-than-to-ask expression. "Her name is Helen Emerson. She sells herself as Mrs. Clean. No one is that clean, if you ask me. I wouldn't trust her as far as I could throw her, and that isn't very far." His gaze strayed back to the Westerfield woman. "This music is inspiring. I think I want to dance."

Jill Westerfield was just breaking away from her politician date. She disappeared back into the crowd, Corbett following. Grace hoped her brother knew what he was doing, consorting with the enemy so to speak.

The enemy…how far would they go? Had Larry Laroche or Helen Emerson paid to have those photos taken of her? Was one of them planning on blackmailing her brother or mother? Grace couldn't let their political careers be hurt because of her…but if Laroche or Emerson was behind the blackmail scheme, how could she stop them?

She would look for an opportunity to talk to the two politicians in question in person tonight.

Would they look at her with practiced politician

expressions? Would one of them have a secret smile behind his eyes? Knowing she would come face-to-face with the person responsible for those photographs made it hard to take a deep breath.

Approaching Larry Laroche, who still stood at the edge of the dance floor, Grace wondered if she could get him off guard.

When she heard him tell a companion, "You just have to find the right weapon, but you can manipulate anyone into doing what you want," she had to fight back the urge to face off with him, right then, right there.

Was his weapon a photograph?

Her mouth went dry and her throat tightened and her feet suddenly felt as if they were filled with lead.

"Excuse me," came a familiar voice, "but I feel as if we've met before."

Starting, Grace glanced to her right to see Declan dressed in a black tux with a black collarless shirt. He was as stunning a man as any in the room. More so. Her heart beat faster even as she took a quick look around. People were watching, so, taking a calming breath, she went along with him.

"Perhaps we've met at another fund-raiser."

"We've met in my dreams—the ones I have after seeing you in those Voodoo ads." He held out his hand. "Dance with me?"

Grace lowered her voice. "I don't want to give

Mama any ideas. If she thinks there's anything going on between us…"

Not that she'd seen Mama yet, but Grace was certain her mother was here somewhere in the crowd.

"Oh, come on, let's give her something to chew on."

As Declan smoothly swung her into his arms and onto the dance floor, Grace couldn't escape his touch without making a scene. She shut down that part of her mind that would seek a vision. Practiced enough at it over the past dozen years, she was relieved when nothing untoward happened. He turned her in his arms, and she glimpsed her brother on the sidelines. No blonde. The Westerfield woman had either gotten away or turned him down. Her loss, Grace thought, as Corbett gave her a thumbs-up.

A moment later, when she was facing her brother again, Mama was next to him. Beaming.

Just great.

She would have to explain Declan, only she didn't know how when she couldn't explain him to herself.

"This isn't a date," Grace reminded him.

"I never said it was."

Dipping her, Declan made her catch her breath. Concentrating on keeping any visions at bay, she was relieved when he pulled her upright.

Then she said, "But you were thinking it."

"How do you know? Are you *psychic?*"

Ignoring the question, she said, "When you came in, I was about to get better acquainted with Larry Laroche, the man running against my brother for the city council seat."

"Now we can do it together."

He put a protective arm around her back and started her through the crowd toward the bar where Laroche held court. They didn't get very far before Mama appeared, beautiful and dignified as always in a navy dress and long-sleeved jacket with crystal buttons that left little uncovered.

"Why, Grace, darlin', aren't you going to introduce me to your young man?"

"He's not mine, Mama. We just met."

Mama's gaze went to Declan's hand at her waist and her eyebrows lifted a notch.

"Declan McKenna," he said, holding out his free hand for a shake. "So nice to meet you, Mrs. Broussard. Or should that be *Judge* Broussard?"

Mama took his hand, saying, "Why, surely it should be and perhaps it shall. Aren't you sweet to make note of my ambition."

"I keep abreast of what's going on in my city."

"Ooh, a potential politician."

"Now you're flattering me."

"What is it you *do,* darlin'?" Mama asked Declan. Grace cut in. "Oh, look, Mama. There's Bitsy Halloway." They hadn't agreed on Declan's cover story and she was anxious to distract her mother. "I think she's looking for you."

Mama turned and waved to the society woman who was staring vacantly their way, then said, "All right, I understand you don't need your mama playing chaperone. You two enjoy yourselves tonight."

With that, Mama headed straight for Bitsy.

"I sense that didn't go well for you."

Clenching her jaw at Declan's amused tone, Grace said, "Mama sees what she wants to see."

"What might that be?"

"Me settled down in an imitation of her."

Grace turned her gaze back to the bar where she spotted both politicians in question. Larry Laroche and Helen Emerson seemed to be in the middle of a disagreement.

"I wonder what they're arguing about."

"I don't know about you," Declan said, guiding her through the crowd, "but I can't eavesdrop from this distance."

Grace let Declan lead her to the other side of the room. "So how do we do this?" she asked.

"Be yourself. Or better yet…be Voodoo Woman."

Thinking Declan was mocking her with the comment, she glared at him but got a blank look in response.

"Did I speak out of turn?"

"No." She shook her head. "You just surprised me

is all." No one had ever told her to be wild and free in quite that way before. Or in any way, come to think of it. Warmth regenerated her. Her spine straightened, her head tilted, her lips curved. She was ready.

As they approached the politicians, Grace concentrated on the heated discussion between Laroche and Emerson.

"Why waste good money on the rug rats?" Laroche was saying. His thin lips were turned down, his beady, dark eyes flashed, his narrow nostrils flared. "High school is soon enough to buy computer equipment."

"I beg to differ." Helen Emerson's face was flushed to the roots of her red hair. "Grammar schools need the newest technology if the poorer children are going to keep up with the ones who have access at home!"

"More'n half of 'em won't finish high school anyhow."

"Not if they're left technologically behind, they won't. That's why it's so important to start them on computers while they're young."

"I'm officially bored by this conversation," Laroche suddenly announced. "I'm bored with this so-called party. We need something to liven it up. I know some very lovely Bourbon Street talent that could do the trick."

So his mind went to the lowest level, Grace thought, more than halfway convinced he was the blackmailer.

"You're inappropriate, as usual," Helen told him.

"If your potential constituents heard you, you wouldn't get elected to dogcatcher."

"You don't really think elections are won on the level of appropriateness, do you?" Laroche snorted. "If so, then you'd better look to the skeletons in your own closet. I could ruin you and you know it."

Helen sputtered, "Y-you're mad! If you dare spread rumors about me, Larry Laroche, you will rue the day you were born!"

"A pretty big threat. Be sure you're up to the truth being disseminated in the most public of ways. Have no doubt I know where the bodies are buried."

Grace was trying not to react to that—did he mean real bodies or was that a metaphor for some other scandal?—when Jill Westerfield entered the fray.

"Larry, there's someone I want you to meet," she said smoothly. "A man of influence, who is interested in supporting you. You'll excuse us, won't you?" she asked Helen.

"By all means," the older woman said. "Go meet the spawn of Satan. That's the only support you'll get in this city."

Just then, Declan grabbed a couple of champagne flutes from a waiter's tray and handed one to Grace.

"To your success as Voodoo Woman," he said loud enough that both politicians turned to look.

Aware that he'd done it on purpose to see what reaction he would get, Grace steeled herself.

"Well, well, look who we have here," Laroche crooned in a sickening voice. "A real *in-the-buff* celebrity."

The way he worded it made Grace want to toss the expensive champagne in his face and then tell him off. Sensing Declan was about to make a move on Laroche, Grace grasped his arm and gave him a look meant to tell him she could handle this.

"And I'll use my celebrity to make sure my brother beats you at the polls hands down," she said, turning his slur on him.

"Why, you bi—"

"Keep a civil tongue in your head!" Helen interrupted. "You are speaking to a lady."

"Lady? Where?"

"Now, Larry, we are in public," the Westerfield woman murmured even as she gave Grace a once-over with an expression that made her skin crawl.

Just then a flash went off.

"Gotcha!" Max Babin was on the move, taking candid shots of the partygoers. The photographer was dressed in a black sequin-trimmed man's tux. "One more time," she said, zeroing in on Laroche. "Everyone smile."

Was that a significant look that passed between the photographer and Laroche? Grace wondered. Did they have some kind of relationship? How many women did he have other than his wife? Her pulse threaded unevenly. What if it wasn't a sexual thing? What if Laroche had paid Max to get those photographs for his blackmail scheme?

As if he could sense her disquiet, Declan found her free hand and squeezed encouragingly.

Unprepared for the unexpected contact, Grace moaned....

He kisses the arch of her bare foot...makes his way up her calf...laves her inner thigh. He hesitates at her entrance, his warmth breath teasing her.

She throws back her head...invites him in...

Another camera flash snapped Grace out of the sensual vision.

"Better be prepared to give your brother a shoulder to cry on when *he* loses." Laroche barked a laugh. "I have a couple of tricks up my sleeve."

"Mr. Porter is waiting," Jill said, this time physically pulling Laroche away.

"I apologize if you were at all offended," Helen said, smiling at Grace. "Helen Emerson."

"Yes, I know who you are, as well."

And she was put off by the way the other woman was looking at her...something odd in her gaze... She was known as Mrs. Clean according to Corbett. But what if that was all for show as he'd suggested?

Grace asked, "So are you as confident as your sparring partner?"

"One can never be too confident in politics. We

just have to trust that the people will take a hard look at the candidates, weed out the *unacceptable* and elect the right people."

Her emphasis on *unacceptable* didn't get by Grace. "Yes, we have to trust that the voters can see through the facade to the *real* person."

Helen's face started turning red again, but rather than arguing, she backed away. "If you'll excuse me, I see someone else I need to charm."

Someone else? Grace was anything *but* charmed.

Declan gave her hand another encouraging squeeze, but this time she kept herself grounded in the present. "I have questions about both of them," he said.

"Me, too. It's a toss-up as to which one *wouldn't* resort to blackmail." Seeing Raphael headed her way with one of his wealthiest clients in tow, Grace smiled and murmured, "Work time."

"Grace," the designer said, "Mrs. Bichoux would like to see you model Raphael's exquisite design."

For some reason, the designer liked to refer to himself by name as if he were speaking of another person. Suddenly she realized Raphael was staring at Declan, who quietly excused himself and melted into the crowd.

Grace nodded at the woman. "Mrs. Bichoux."

"Oh, the gown is so lovely. I can almost see myself dancing in it."

The older woman's face was lit with expectation,

so Grace turned slowly and showed off the little details that made one of Raphael's gowns so special.

Then he snapped to and turned his attention back to his client. "You like Raphael's newest treasure?"

"It's wonderful, as all your creations are, of course, dear Raphael."

"It will be wonderful on you."

"Maybe…"

Mrs. Bichoux didn't sound as convinced that it was for her as she had at first. And it really wasn't. Way too much skin showing for the mature, well-rounded client. Grace couldn't believe Raphael would allow a client to wear something that wouldn't accentuate the positive. What was the designer thinking?

"Raphael, may I speak to you for a moment?"

Her employer turned to face her and annoyance quickly crossed his features. "But of course." He grasped her elbow and pulled her away from Mrs. Bichoux. "What is it?"

"Mrs. Bichoux is a lovely woman, but this particular gown won't flatter her rather mature figure. What about the pale blue—"

"Are you questioning my judgment?"

"I know you want your clients to be happy—"

"So if Mrs. Bichoux wants this gown, she shall have it."

Raphael's tone was clipped, making Grace take a step back. "Yes, of course."

Grace stared at him. He'd never spoken to her like this before. As a matter of fact, in the past, he'd sought out and had valued her opinion.

What was going on with him? Was he so desperate to make a big sale that he'd intentionally foist an unsuitable gown on a wealthy client?

What else would Raphael do to make some fast money?

Chapter Six

More than an hour later, Grace entered Declan's apartment, wondering if she'd made a mistake in letting him talk her into waiting there for the e-mail to come through.

Raphael had exhausted her by making her show the gown off for one woman at a time. It seemed every one of his local clients had been at the fundraiser. A lot of potentials, too. And Raphael had seemed determined to sell the gown to every one of them. Grace had remained gracious when she'd wanted more than anything to leave. She still couldn't figure out where Raphael's antagonism had come from.

Now she was simply wiped out. And tense.

She tried distracting herself by taking a good look around. The living area was huge, the kitchen separated from the rest of the room by a black granite-topped breakfast bar. The kitchen cabinetry was black, the appliances stainless steel. In the living area, the leather seating was black as was a baby grand piano. Declan's place was so neat and orderly, obviously like him and unlike her.

Running her fingers lightly over the piano keys, she asked, "You play?"

"Not nearly well enough. I noodle around once in a while, but I haven't actually had a lesson since I was a kid."

"But you bought the piano."

"Actually, my grandmother left it to me. She always hoped I would take up music again. Not enough time. It's the only thing I brought with me when I moved from New Mexico."

She'd wondered where he was from—his accent betrayed him—but she couldn't focus on the fact. "It's almost midnight."

"Afraid you'll turn into a pumpkin?"

"I did that years ago. It's not me I'm worried about."

Not totally, anyway. She'd survived scandal and innuendo more than once. Only before, it had never been bad enough to reflect on Mama and Corbett. She couldn't stop thinking about them, about her possibly destroying everything they'd worked for without even trying.

"So let's go into my office."

Grace followed Declan into a black-and-white reflection of the living area. She couldn't help wondering if his bedroom was equally colorless. The computer was running. Declan hit the space bar and the monitor sprang to life.

"Go ahead and bring up your e-mail program." He slid the chair out from under the desk for her.

Grace nodded and sat. She brought up her e-mail program and gave it a quick check.

"Nothing yet. There's still a few minutes until midnight." She rose and fiddled with the mouse. "Distract me." She didn't want to keep rehashing negative thoughts in her mind.

"Your wish," Declan murmured, stepping closer. His expression read neutral, but she recognized his intention.

Her breath catching and a thrill racing through her, Grace nevertheless put out a staying hand. Her palm burned against his chest.

He falls back onto the black satin bedspread and brings her with him. He grows hard against her stomach as he kisses her and cups her breasts....

Pulling herself out of the fantasy, Grace snapped back her hand. "I meant talk to me."

He grinned. "About?"

That smile made her go all soft inside, but she was good at hiding what she didn't want others to know. "Tell me about your family," she said. "You know all about mine. I know nothing about yours."

"A father, three younger brothers and one sister,

several aunts and uncles and dozens of cousins. All-in-all, a big, messy family."

"Are they still in New Mexico?"

He nodded. "My parents, sister and one of my brothers."

"So why did you leave?"

"Personal reasons."

Which meant a woman, Grace thought. But before she could tactfully ask about it, he went on.

"My cousin Ian has been a private investigator for several years. He worked for a big firm, mostly on court cases, and he was itching to start his own business. So we fell into it together."

"You were a private investigator in New Mexico?"

"Police detective. But enough about me. What about you? How did you become Voodoo Woman?"

So why was he avoiding telling her about New Mexico? Grace wondered. There *had* to be a woman in the story he wasn't telling. And if he couldn't talk about it, he wasn't over it yet.

She said, "I took a long, circuitous route. I never got a degree and I didn't have a career, so when the opportunity came along, I jumped on it. I was impressed by Raphael's clothing and introduced him to some of his current clients and the next thing I knew he asked me to work for him."

"You didn't like school?"

She shrugged. "It was…unsatisfying. I wanted to

find myself. I keep thinking I should go back… finish…but I don't know any universities that give degrees in what I do."

"But maybe you could get a degree in something related that would appeal to you. Fashion. Or marketing."

There it was—dissatisfaction with who she was. No big surprise. Grace turned away and moved to the windows with their view of the Mississippi River.

"A degree isn't the most important thing in life."

"No, not if you're productively employed and happy."

Not appreciating the direction of the conversation, she suddenly felt the walls closing in on her. "I was just thinking…maybe I should go back to my place while I still have time."

"Why would you want to leave?"

Straight-faced, she asked, "What if the blackmailer demands I meet him near my building?"

"We're less than ten minutes away by car." Declan used reason to convince her to stay. "I can't see him asking to meet you face-to-face. And even if he did, I wouldn't let you, not alone."

"Wouldn't let me?" she echoed, liking the way the conversation was headed less and less.

"Isn't that what you hired me to do—protect you?"

Grace didn't want to argue, and truth be told, she

desperately needed backup. If only he hadn't started to sound like her brother. Or worse, her mother.

Resigning herself to staying, she couldn't help but pace the room until a ding from the computer alerted her to the arrival of e-mail. Her heart thumped and her mouth went dry and she stood frozen for a moment.

THE SUBJECT LINE SIMPLY READ *Photographs* like it was a normal message from a friend. What had they expected? Declan wondered. That the bastard who sent it would identify the e-mail as *Blackmail?*

Grace sat and clicked on the blackmailer's e-mail. Declan held his breath and read along with her:

I HOPE YOU LIKE THE PHOTOGRAPH I SENT YOU. I HAVE DOZENS OF OTHER SHOTS, ALL EQUALLY HOT. YOU CAN EITHER BUY THEM FROM ME OR I CAN SELL THEM TO THE TABLOIDS AND RUIN YOUR FAMILY. YOU HAVE 72 HOURS TO COME UP WITH FIVE HUNDRED THOUSAND DOLLARS IN CASH. WATCH FOR FURTHER INSTRUCTIONS VIA E-MAIL MIDNIGHT TOMORROW.

Grace gasped. "Five hundred thousand dollars? He's out of his mind!"

Her fingers flew over the keyboard as she replied:

I don't have that kind of money.

Declan placed a comforting hand on her shoulder. He could feel Grace's turmoil churning through her, but she didn't say anything. They waited together silently, tensely. A moment later, a ding accompanied the blackmailer's reply. She clicked on the e-mail. The response was simple:

GET IT!

Which reminded Declan of *Gotcha!* Declan wondered if Max Babin might have several businesses like this going on the side.

"Get it how?" Though Grace whispered, she sounded panicky.

"You're not really thinking of trying to pay off a blackmailer?"

"What else am I supposed to do?" Quickly she typed:

You're crazy if you think I would give you a cent even if I had it to give. Which I don't!

Though she froze in front of the screen waiting for a response, none came.

When Grace turned to him, her expression was stricken. She pushed herself away from the desk and stumbled to her feet. Declan caught her and held her comfortingly, his hand smoothing the tension from her spine. For a moment, she melted against him.

Then, as if she rethought what they were doing, Grace pushed against his chest until he let go of her. She had that odd expression again, the one he kept seeing when they connected.

"Sorry," he said, allowing worry to enter both his voice and his expression. "I didn't mean to offend you."

"You didn't. It's just…when you touch me, I get these flashes…"

"What kind of flashes?"

"Of us…together."

"I'm flattered."

"Don't be. It's some kind of psychic malfunction."

"So you *are* psychic." He'd wondered how long it would take her to admit it.

"Not actively psychic though. Not for years. Not until I walked into your office."

"You're saying *I'm* responsible."

"No. It's not your fault. It's mine. I guess I relaxed my guard or something."

"Maybe that's good."

"No, not good. Bad. Very bad. I thought I was done with that stuff."

"So you've been repressing your gift." Just as did

some of the McKennas, Declan thought. Not that he ever had reason to do so. But she must. "Why?"

"I didn't want to be publicly humiliated again," Grace admitted. "And it's not a gift." She turned away from him, mumbling, "It's a damn curse!"

He doubted she knew about curses, not the way he did. He doubted she'd ever left a man she'd cared about to protect him. Realizing she wasn't going to tell him more unless he prodded, he asked, "A family ability?"

"Sort of. Not Mama or Corbett. They would never allow themselves to go off in some fanciful direction. My grandmama Madelaine had it. And Cousin Minny."

Grace was pacing, working herself up into a tight ball of stress, but Declan knew she had to get some of her frustration out. And the more he knew, the more likely he could help her. "Cousin Minny?"

"My eccentric cousin who runs a little shop off Jackson Square. She reads palms and auras and tarot. The tourists love her."

"Sounds like she loves what she does for a living."

Grace nodded. "She's very colorful and theatrical. I'm nothing like her."

Declan couldn't suppress a smile. "Uh-huh."

"Let's get back to the problem at hand. Ferreting out the rat who's trying to ruin my family."

"If his goal was to ruin your mother's or brother's

political career, he could already have sold the photographs to the tabloids."

"But he wouldn't get half a million."

"He could be some sleazy lowlife just trying to make easy money."

"Or not." She made a sound that expressed her frustration. "It's not like Mama's running for mayor or governor. Not Corbett, either. I make pretty good money—I don't even have to buy my own clothes— but I don't make enough to save that much. This blackmailer has no idea…"

"Or assumes you have family money."

"My trust fund doesn't kick in for another year."

They had to nail the blackmailer and any accomplices. And then he had to convince her to take it to the authorities.

"Maybe the blackmailer knows about the trust fund but not that you don't have access. Maybe he thinks five hundred thousand is reasonable, small enough that you wouldn't take the chance of going to the police."

"But we don't know that he isn't hand-in-hand with Laroche or Emerson."

"No, we don't know that. What if this guy is working for one of them but has decided to make a little extra on the side? You get the disk or whatever media the guy stored the photos on— and then find out he was a shill for someone else who has copies he's planning to distribute to the media anyway?"

Grace groaned. "What am I going to do?" She stared at him for a moment unblinking, as if her head was whirling with possibilities. "I still don't want to deal with anything psychic."

"It sounds like you're already doing it. With me."

"Against my will."

Declan stepped closer and was hard pressed not to take her in his arms and make more of those psychic visions right now. "You've done things with me against your will?"

Grace flushed with attractive color. "Only in my head."

He let go a low whistle. "I'd sure like to take a look in there."

"It's not funny!"

Realizing he was upsetting rather than relaxing her with a little humor, Declan immediately sobered. "Sorry. You need to think about going to the authorities, though. We only have seventy-two hours to figure out who is involved and why, and get our hands on those photo files."

"I told you I don't want to bring in the police."

Stubborn woman. Not that Declan could blame her. She was used to having control over her life. Once she brought in the authorities, her life wouldn't be her own.

"Okay," he said, "it's your decision. Only…how does our knowing who the blackmailer is resolve the situation?"

"I'll *threaten* to go to the police."

"And you think someone who has stalked and blackmailed you will believe that considering you didn't do that from the start?"

"Then I'll think of something else. I'll reason with him, convince him I don't have the money. Give him what I have."

Declan didn't want to argue with her. He'd planted the thought in her head. For the moment, that would have to suffice. Eventually she would get that she was in a no-win situation. There was really nothing she could do other than to get her hands on half a million dollars and hope handing it over would stop the blackmailer from spreading her photographs. Or against her will, she could bring in the authorities who would arrest him and bring him to trial.

Changing the subject, he said, "Tomorrow I'll need that list of workers in your building."

"Fine. I'll get it for you."

"Meanwhile, I'll see what I can do about tracking the blackmailer down through his e-mail. If we do find him…well, it's something to sleep on."

"Sleep." Grace sighed. "I could use some of that."

"The bed's right in the next room."

"Alone."

Though Declan could be persuaded to sleep with the woman—easily, in fact—that's not what he'd been suggesting. "I'll take you home."

"Not necessary."

"I know you're probably used to doing everything on your own, but this is one time when you could use someone watching your back."

Thankfully, she didn't argue.

Declan didn't usually use his car in this part of the city, but it was too late to walk or take public transportation, and he knew getting a taxi in the middle of the night might take some doing. So he broke out the SUV from the garage and drove. Grace remained quiet all the way to Faubourg-Marigny—her adrenaline seemed to have run out.

As it was, she seemed to be half-asleep already. Her head rested against the seat back and was turned his way. Waiting at a red light at Jackson Square, he glanced over at her. Her eyes were closed and he could hear her breathing.

Even at this hour, an old guy was playing his sax for tips outside of Café du Monde. The sound made Declan yearn for something he couldn't quite name. The music swelled and it took him a moment to realize his chest had pulled tight and he was white-knuckling the steering wheel.

Sexual tension, he told himself, that was all this was. He couldn't remember the last time he'd been with a woman. Sometime before Lila. Nearly a year. While he'd fallen for Lila and she'd told him she wanted him, he hadn't been willing to put her in danger. To subject her to the family curse.

But a man had needs….

He looked away from Grace and the very second the light turned green, he took off as if he could run away from something too scary to consider.

A few minutes later, he was pulling up to her building. He parked and said, "Hey, sleepyhead, we're here."

Grace started awake and for a moment seemed confused. Then her forehead smoothed out and she sighed. "I must have fallen asleep."

"You're exhausted. Let's get you upstairs."

"You don't need to see me up."

"My mother taught me better."

Nodding, she let him open the downstairs door for her. He stayed behind her, glued to the sway of her hips as he followed her up the stairs. By the time they reached the door, he was aching for her. When she fumbled for the keys, he took them from her and unlocked the door.

"I should come in, make sure you're safe."

An excuse, of course. He didn't want to leave her yet. He recognized that he was making a mistake wanting her. She was a client. He had to keep the case uppermost in his mind.

Preceding her into the apartment, Declan turned on the lights and looked around. Her living area was colorful and messy. Mango walls with some wild if unrelated art pieces and an assortment of furnishings including a gold-trimmed peacock-blue chest and leopard-print chaise all made him feel Grace bought each piece on impulse. Considering what she did for a living, she must know decorators who could pull the apartment together perfectly. And yet what he saw fit the woman. He liked it and he liked her.

Thinking he should leave, he stopped when he noted her expression.

"I don't want to do it," she suddenly announced, her face frozen in an expression of panic. "But I don't see any other way."

"Don't want to do what?"

"Read people, to learn their intentions. Raphael and Max. Larry Laroche and Helen Emerson."

"You're talking about using that psychic ability you've kept at bay for years?" When she gave him a disbelieving look, he added, "Using your ability could get you into trouble…perhaps put you in a dangerous situation."

"I know," she said.

He realized she was thinking about her reason for suppressing her ability, whatever that might be. Knowing having a gift wasn't always easy made him feel for her.

Her expression tight, Grace choked out, "But what if using my psychic ability is the only way to get to the truth?"

Declan's gut twisted. "Or it may be the way to get in deep trouble. I don't think you should involve yourself that way, Grace," he said, stepping closer. He shouldn't feel so personally involved with a client, but he couldn't help himself. He liked Grace Broussard and didn't want anything bad to happen to her. "Put yourself out as bait and you could get hurt."

"What if it's the only way?" she asked again.

"We'll think of something," he assured her. "Get the money—disk trade on our terms and then nail the bastard—"

"I don't think that's going to work. I've spent a lifetime denying my ability so I would be like everyone else. Maybe I should make an exception in this case."

Declan smiled. "Do you really think you're like anyone else? You've had the courage to do what many people wouldn't. You've explored life— schools, majors, jobs—until you found something that made you happy. Most people do what they think they should and live narrow, unhappy lives."

Her emotions surrounded him like a tight glove. He sensed fear and despair and determination, plus something else he couldn't quite name. The sensation suddenly amped up and he was caught by the tension gripping Grace. A tension that was only for him.

He could feel it…her wanting him.

Unable to help himself, he stepped closer.

Chapter Seven

Touched that Declan appreciated what Mama and her social set had always criticized, Grace thought that she could care about this man. She already felt more connected to him than anyone in her past. The visions had to be responsible—she hadn't known him long enough to form real feelings. Had she? She simply knew she wanted his arms around her, wanted to feel protected for once in her life.

Without thinking, she slipped her hands up his chest and around his neck and swayed into him. And for a moment, she went still as her heart fluttered and her belly knotted. Then she felt his hand on her spine, rubbing her soothingly, like he would a cat. Nothing sexual there.

Only she was seeing it…

He bends over and she feels the warmth of his mouth on her flesh. Wet kisses trail over her shoulders and down the length of her spine.

Her flesh pebbled.

Grace didn't understand how this could be happening. How did she keep seeing these sexual videos of the two of them inside her head? Maybe it was because she wanted—no, needed—Declan. He was not only desirable, but a man a woman could count on for help. She was certain he would do everything in his power to make this horrible situation go away for her.

Besides, she was the woman in the secret photograph.

No matter how humiliated she would be if the photo got out, Grace knew the blackmailer had captured a small part of the real her, the part that mostly played inside her own head. She hadn't been with a man for so long that she yearned for it. Yearned for Declan McKenna.

Maybe if she gave way to her want, she would stop having these visions. Maybe they were simply echoes of desire rather than psychic encounters.

When Declan lowered his head, she raised hers for his kiss.

His teeth catch her lower lip and worry it until she gasps with pleasure. Then he covers her mouth and she feels herself drown in his kiss.

Grace took a deep breath. She didn't know which was better—reality or the visions playing havoc with her senses.

On top, she rocks, his hands splayed over her hips. Then one moves down toward the center, and suddenly his fingers play with what his erection can't reach.

He kissed her again. Vision and reality blended as he stroked her through the dress. Her breasts responded instantly. It had been too long and she was too ready to be with a man to protest. Breathless, she was on fire.

Maybe Declan could stop her from remembering the photograph, remembering she was being stalked and blackmailed.

Wanting that more than anything, she urged, "Take me."

"Are you sure?"

"Don't talk." She led him to the edge of the sofa. "Just make everything else go away."

Declan turned her and ran his lips up her spine… just like in the first vision.

He slipped the dress from her shoulders, then turned her again and as the material flowed downward, caught one nipple and drew it deep into his mouth until she felt a warm, thick flood between her thighs. His touch there was soft and all too seductive.

Shuddering with desire, Grace undid his belt and opened the front of his trousers. He was long and heavy and hot in her hand. He groaned and kissed her, pushing her back on the couch so they lay length to length, never once stopping the friction that was threatening to spill her over the edge. Then he slipped inside her…she arched and pulled him closer.

Forehead to forehead, they quickened their rhythm. Remembering fantasizing about him in the dressing room, Grace hung on only by a thread. She reveled in the moment, the feel of male flesh—of Declan. His heat was comforting. She felt as if he could shelter her from anything. From bad memories.

Even from a blackmailer.

SO THE PHOTOGRAPHS HAD revealed the truth: Grace Broussard really was a slut.

Watching the action from a window across the street through the French doors of her apartment was like having a wet dream…hot and steamy if not exactly real.

Too bad there was no concealed camera in the apartment to get all the details. To record her in action. But who could have guessed?

Next time.

If Grace thought she could get out of paying, she'd better think again. How dare she say she wasn't going to cooperate and give over the money?

There was more than one way to punish someone who refused.

When all was said and done, when the money

was in more worthy hands, the Broussards would be destroyed.

Every one of them.

IT WAS SOMETIME LATER when Declan's head cleared enough that he questioned what had happened between him and Grace. A frisson of guilt slid through him. She was a client, he reminded himself again, not his woman. That's all that was bothering him. It had nothing to do with the witch's prophecy. It couldn't unless he had deeper feelings for her, which he didn't.

"I probably should leave," he told her, slipping off the sofa and pulling on his pants.

"Right. I have a couple of appointments tomorrow, the first fairly early." Pulling a coverlet around herself, Grace seemed ready to get rid of him. "I could use some sleep. I probably won't be free until late afternoon."

Declan knew it was for the best. He needed a clear head to run this investigation, and it would be easier to get back on track if he had some alone time himself. Maybe she felt the same, the reason her nerves fluttered around him. He finished dressing in record time.

"I'll work on the e-mail, see if there is any way we can trace it back to the source."

"Is that likely?"

"I won't know until I try. I'll also start digging into the lives of our suspects, see what I can get on them."

"Good." Grace was avoiding looking at him directly.

The awkwardness between them grew. He studied her for a moment—took in every detail of her inviting, disheveled appearance, so like her inviting, disheveled apartment. She really was lovely. Warm. Appealing. He had to tear himself from the room. She trailed after him to the front door, the cover wrapped tightly around her. He wanted to take her in his arms and kiss her, but he could feel her mentally pushing him away. She was putting up barriers. Ones he wouldn't cross.

"Call me when you're free then," he said, "and I'll update you—assuming I have anything."

He raced down the stairs. They'd barely met, but it was as if they'd known each other for a very long time. At least he felt that way.

He was feeling other things, things he had to deny. He couldn't care about her, not in *that* way.

Even so, he couldn't keep the prophecy out of his head.

...should they act on their feelings, they will put their loved ones in mortal danger...

But he didn't love Grace, so she was safe, he assured himself, beating back the whisper of guilt that flitted through him. Bad enough that he'd lost his mother to the family curse. He would never take the chance of putting another woman he cared about in that position. He liked Grace, was drawn to her, wanted to protect her, whatever that took. Thankfully, he would never fall in love with her.

If only she wasn't tying his hands about bringing in the authorities, they could wind up this case fast and go their own ways. Then there would be no chance of feelings between them developing.

His head was whirling with things he needed to do to help Grace as he stepped out into the street. Suddenly his instincts kicked in and he knew he wasn't alone. It was the middle of the night—some drunk stumbling home from a club? But that's not what he sensed.

Waves of anger assaulted him. On guard, he stopped and looked around for the source. The area was dark but for pools of light from the streetlamps. The emotions enveloping him seemed to be coming from across the way...from a shadowy doorway. Whoever was hidden there had a direct line of sight to the building, and, he realized when he glanced over his shoulder, to Grace's apartment.

Just then, Grace stepped onto the balcony, as if she wanted to look for him. He waved, then she stiffened and stepped back, closed the door, then the curtain. And in that instant, anger and contempt from the watcher intensified.

"Hey, you!" Declan yelled, realizing this could be Grace's stalker and blackmailer. "What do you think you're doing?"

The hidden watcher burst free of the shadows, the dark figure flying down the street. On automatic, Declan followed, but wasn't fast enough to catch up. The guy turned a corner and, determined not to lose him, Declan forced himself to go faster. Relieved when he picked up the trail, Declan tried to get a better look at the guy. Dressed in dark clothes, he was wearing a billed cap that shadowed his face. He wasn't a big guy, probably the reason he was so fast.

The guy took the Esplanade like a kamikaze, weaving in and out of traffic as if defying death. Declan hesitated long enough to catch a breath and thankfully the light changed. He lunged across Esplanade and then down Royal Street into the heart of the French Quarter.

Drawing on his reserves to catch up, Declan picked up speed, turned a couple of corners onto Bourbon Street where revelers got between him and his prey—the guy ducked between a musician beating on a drum and a couple coming out of a bar carrying drinks in plastic cups.

And then he simply vanished.

His chest heaving, Declan stood in one spot for a moment and tried to pierce the crowd. No use.

He'd lost him! Damn!

Unsure of what the stalker might do next— whether or not he would return and try to get to Grace—Declan returned to his car. There he hunkered down to wait.

Just in case.

Chapter Eight

After spending half the night thinking about Declan, Grace awoke Sunday morning only to think of him some more. Part of her realized they never should have slept together. She didn't even know him…and yet part of her felt she did. Still, the action had been foolish, prompted by the need to be comforted, to find safe shelter as her world dissolved around her. In the heat of the moment, what she'd done had seemed natural. She'd been drawn to Declan's strength and kindness. She had no expectations, no reason to wonder if he might disappoint her in the future.

Her trust was not easily won.

A cold shower couldn't make her put Declan out of mind. She couldn't forget about him, couldn't forget how he'd seemed to really care that she was safe, couldn't forget the instant connection between them. By the time she was dry, she was perspiring again. Hopefully, her Sunday newspaper and a fresh pot of coffee would set her on the right track. Lots and lots of coffee.

The caffeine would brace her for a few hours with Mama and Corbett.

Since Daddy had died several years ago, Mama had started a family tradition—a monthly Sunday brunch where she caught up with her children's lives. They couldn't even meet in neutral territory at a restaurant. Mama insisted her children come to the Garden District family mansion, where they ate in the formal dining room, a reminder for Grace of too many years of repressive living.

She chose a flirty purple number from her new wardrobe, even knowing her mother would be sure to lift an eyebrow. Mama rarely commented anymore, but Grace still imagined her disapproval every time. No doubt Mama would like to see her dressed in a nun's habit.

As if clothes really made the woman. She guessed that was what bugged her the most—Mama making such a big deal over lifestyle choices that had nothing to do with who she was as a person. She loved her mother and knew Mama loved her equally in return. Maybe all mothers and daughters were at odds. And maybe if Daddy was still alive, Mama would be fussing over him instead of her only daughter.

GRACE ARRIVED at the Broussard family home at a little before nine. The thought of the photograph uppermost on her mind, she dreaded stepping through the white columns of the veranda to the twelve-foot-high double front doors. She feared that somehow, Mama or Corbett would wrest the blackmail scheme from her.

Entering the atrium foyer, she called out, "Where is everyone?" and plastered a smile to her lips.

"In here, darlin'."

Grace made her way back through the antique-laden parlor and dining room to the more modern solarium with its wicker and glass furniture.

"Ah, there you are."

Dressed in a skirt suit and plain pumps that she might wear in a courtroom while prosecuting a case, Sandra Broussard set down a watering can and stepped out from a forest of plants. There was a small but lush private garden out back—Mama's personal pride and joy.

Fussing with her already perfectly coifed dark hair, she said, "Your brother arrived half an hour ago. I was wondering if you were still asleep."

Grace merely smiled, gave her mother a hug and kissed her cheek. "Nice to see you, too, Mama."

Mama had no clue as to how hard she worked, how little she played, Grace knew. The parties she went to with Raphael were a bit of both, but she had to be "on" every moment to sell whatever design of his that she was wearing that evening. She loved being part of something so exciting, on the threshold of exploding into a national or even international business, but sometimes Grace wished she could relax and simply have a good time.

"If you lived here where you belong," Mama said, "time wouldn't be an issue."

"I'm sure we'd have other issues," Grace said, turning to Corbett.

"Hey, sis." He set down his newspaper, then rose from his club chair to give her a hug and to whisper in her ear. "Don't let her get to you today."

"About what?" she whispered in return.

Corbett pulled away and just rolled his eyes.

Dear Lord, had they found out about the photographs of her? If so, she would be humiliated, and to make it even worse, would undoubtedly get a lecture on the consequences of what they saw as her wild lifestyle.

But when she glanced at her mother, Sandra Broussard wore an expression like the cat who'd swallowed the cream. Uh-oh, it seemed she was *still* in trouble, if of a different kind. Grace took a deep breath and waited for it.

"Would you like something cool to refresh you?" Mama asked, drawing out her words. "Sweet tea or freshly squeezed lemonade, same as always, darlin'.

Unless you have something to celebrate. Then I might be in mind to have Cornelia open a bottle of champagne and make us all mimosas."

Grace narrowed her gaze at Mama. "And what might I be celebrating?"

"A *suitable* new man in your life."

Grace didn't miss the emphasis on the word *suitable,* which meant Mama approved. Even though she knew, Grace asked, "Now who would you be talking about?"

"Declan McKenna, of course. Now, what is it he does for a living?"

Uh-oh, they'd never come up with a cover story for him. Trying not to panic, Grace changed the direction of the conversation.

"Whatever makes you think he's the new man in my life, Mama? I just met him yesterday."

"I am not blind, Grace Broussard. I saw the way the two of you danced together."

"Well, then, send out the wedding announcements."

Corbett coughed and Grace gave him a wicked glare. She could tell her brother was trying not to laugh.

"If it was just the dance, I might be hopeful but yearning for more." Mama lifted the pitcher of lemonade and filled a glass. "As it is, Hattie Babineaux said the two of you were together all night.

She said his arm was around you...*well!*...quite possessively. And that you left *early*."

Hattie Babbles-a-lot, as Corbett called her, had always seemed to be a font of information on everyone's activities. The woman had tattled on Grace the first time she'd worn makeup without permission at the age of fourteen. Grace swore the society gossip had spies all over the city.

"Hattie has too much time on her hands."

"Grace! Are you telling me there is nothing going on between you and Declan?"

Feeling as if someone had put a camera in her apartment and had shared the footage with Mama, Grace gaped at her a moment before grabbing the drink and turning to her brother who couldn't quite hide his smirk.

"So how is your love life, Corbett? Seeing anyone suitable that you can bring home to Mama?" she asked, knowing he'd gone gun-shy after the Naomi disaster.

"Now why are you picking on me?"

"Because you think it's funny."

"You've always had the power to amuse and entertain, Grace."

"You didn't answer my question."

"No, I surely didn't." He grinned openly at her.

And Grace let it go for the moment. If Corbett had succeeded in cornering Jill Westerfield the night before, he kept it to himself. The question was, how would he keep it from Hattie and Mama, much less the media?

As a politician, anything he did was fair game—they would report anyone he was seeing, suitable or not. And considering the woman had some kind of relationship with his friend, the media would have a field day. Though not as big a field day as the press would have if they got hold of those photographs.

"Your brother is too busy working on his next campaign to get involved with anyone," Mama said.

Corbett nodded vigorously, but Grace noted the same sparkle in his eyes that he'd had when watching the Westerfield woman the night before. Her brother had a secret wild streak of his own that played against his conservative image. He was simply more clever than she at keeping it hidden. He was all about appearances. His. Mama's. Unfortunately, hers.

He would never have to worry about inappropriate photos of *him* making the rounds.

Which brought her worry to the surface. Grace simply didn't believe Raphael was involved, even if he did need money. Or Max. More likely, politics was the catalyst. That meant someone who had it in for Mama or Corbett.

"So, make any new enemies lately?" Grace asked, including both in the direct question. "I mean, other than Larry Laroche or Helen Emerson."

"Enemies?" Mama sounded a tad shocked.

"You know, people who don't like you or what you do? Or maybe you've never had that kind of pressure."

"Of course not! Now where is that Cornelia?" Mama asked no one in particular. Frowning, she was already on her way out of the solarium. "I'll go see what's keeping her."

Leave it to Mama to ignore a question that made her uncomfortable.

"What's going on?" Corbett asked. "That's the second time in two days that you asked whether we had enemies. Is that because *you* do?"

"Of course not."

"Grace Madelaine Broussard, you're lying."

"How would you know? You're not psychic."

Thankfully, or he would know the truth. Or as much of it as she knew. Hopefully, Declan would come through and she would soon have the identity of the blackmailer. Until then, she would keep her own counsel.

Knowing the only way to get him off the subject was to change it, she asked, "So what about you and Jill Westerfield? Are you going to pursue the woman?"

"Maybe I already have."

Grace studied her brother. That gleam in his eyes told her what he wouldn't say. "This time, be careful."

"No woman is ever going to use me again the way Naomi did. If anyone is going to do the using—and enjoy it thoroughly—that will be me. Do me a favor—if you find out anything about Jill, keep it to yourself."

"If I kept what I learned about Naomi to myself, you might not still have a career in politics."

While Corbett had been crazy about Naomi, the reporter had slept with him to get information for a story—something she had done with a series of men before. Grace had been the one to get the information on the unethical woman and had immediately shared the news with her brother. Corbett had ended the relationship and had gone to Naomi's editor—a personal friend of his—who had in turn fired the reporter.

The reminder of how badly relationships could end made Grace take stock of whatever it was she had with Declan. Unlike her brother's former lover, Declan was caring and honest. She should be able to trust him.

So what was holding her back?

IT WASN'T UNTIL after he'd followed Grace to a mansion in the Garden District and decided she was safe that Declan headed for home. His vigil had been for naught. The creep he'd chased hadn't returned.

Part of him was glad because that meant Grace was safe for the moment. Part of him wished he could have caught the guy and put a quick end to the blackmail. Though without involving the authorities, he wasn't certain how that scenario was supposed to go. Not that he even knew the guy was in on the blackmail scheme. He simply could have been casing the joint—a simple thief.

Then again, why would a thief have oozed such hostility when he looked at Grace unless it was somehow personal?

Swinging open the door to his condo, Declan slung his tux jacket over a nearby black leather chair. His mind was already churning over the investigation. Finding answers alone might be possible, but the time frame was tight. If he was going to save Grace from the humiliation she so obviously feared, he was going to need help.

There were a hundred ways to spoof information to the recipient. Everything on the Internet could be traced back to its original source if the person looking had the time. No doubt the e-mail header had been spoofed. He opened the properties window that held the full header of the e-mail and found the real Internet service provider the blackmailer had used to send his missive.

If only he had some real skills, he could hack into the ISP and look up the information he needed—he loosely knew the process even if he'd never done the job himself. That would give him the location of the blackmailer's computer when he sent the e-mail. Unfortunately, the company wouldn't give up that information without police intimidation, or more likely a court order. And Grace refused to allow him to go to the police.

If he could get to the receiving mail server, he could look for the logs that would reveal the sending location. Maybe he should try to get to someone at the ISP. More often than not, people were the key to everything. Now he just needed to find someone who knew someone there.

Believing the six degrees of separation rule usually did work, Declan decided to call his cousin Kevin, the computer nerd of the McKenna family.

AFTER BRUNCH, her dilemma in mind, Grace went straight to the French Quarter to visit Minny. It was barely half past eleven and a closed sign hung in the door. The shop didn't open until noon. Grace was thinking about getting a cup of coffee when the door swung wide and Cousin Minny stood there with a big, knowing smile that sent immediate discomfort down Grace's spine. Minny was dressed all in lime-green today—she looked as if she would glow in the dark.

"I knew you were coming," Minny said as Grace entered the store and hugged her cousin.

"Oh, come on. I'm not one of your tourists."

Minny's red eyebrows arched. "You're here to tune up your powers."

"Read that in your crystal ball?"

"Tarot." Minny wrapped an arm around Grace's

back and led her through the front of the store with its magical tourist trinkets to a curtained recessed area near the back room. "Don't worry, Grace, you haven't offended me."

"Sorry," Grace said anyway.

Minny stepped through the gauzy curtains and sat with her back to the wall draped with purple cloth. The little round table was covered in purple, as well. And then over that, Minny had set more gauzy material encrusted with tiny sparkly stars and moons. Not exactly the place to have a serious conversation with her cousin, but objecting would start things off wrong. So Grace sat. Despite what Minny said about the Tarot, she was certain her cousin had simply been expecting her since her visit to the studio.

"So how is he?" Minny asked. "Declan."

"Fine."

"Not what I meant, Grace. Is he as good in person as in your visions?"

"I'm not here to talk about my sex life. Or Declan *per se.*"

"Really? Then you are having sex now? I knew it!"

Flushing, Grace ignored the question. There was no way Minny could be certain of it. "If your tarot told you I was coming, shouldn't it have said why?"

"It's not always that specific. You *are* here about your gift, aren't you?"

"If you want to call it that."

Cousin Minny beamed. "I knew you couldn't ignore it forever."

"I'm desperate."

"Desperate…but not about Declan?" The beam dimmed and Minny's expression became oddly serious. "What, then?"

Grace jumped right in. "Remember the bad-vibes bustier you warned me not to wear?"

"Black with magenta ribbons."

"You were right. I don't think it would really have mattered what I wore, but that was the one…"

"What happened?"

Grace told her. About the photograph…the blackmail…the hidden camera. About thinking Mom's or Corbett's political opponent might be behind the scheme. About her having hired Declan and his certainty the guilty person was some low-level criminal out for a fast buck.

"You aren't going to pay the blackmailer, are you?" Minny asked.

Her cousin's concerned expression wasn't quite the outrage Grace had expected. "I'd thought to— not that I actually have the money, but I was going to try to find it somewhere."

"But not now."

"Declan talked me out of it."

"Good man."

"Except that I still need to deal with the problem

somehow. Starting with figuring out who did it and why, which presents another problem."

"Which you can solve by using your gift, the reason you're here."

Feeling defeated, Grace nodded. "The problem being I don't know how anymore."

"Have you tried?"

"Not really."

"Then how do you know you can't do it?"

Grace shrugged. "I don't get anything off anyone just by touching them. Not a vision into the future, not into their thoughts, not anything."

"Except Declan."

"Except him."

"Hmm. But you haven't really been trying to tune into your visions, right?"

"No. I don't even know where to start."

"Touch me and concentrate."

Grace touched Minny's arm and focused on her cousin's face. "Sorry, nothing."

"Concentrate on something specific you want to know."

Grace thought about Minny's upcoming vacation but she couldn't see Minny anywhere but in New Orleans. "It's not working."

"You just need to practice."

"On whom?"

"On anyone. Practice makes perfect."

"So I touch someone and then just concentrate on that person?"

"Right."

"And if that doesn't work?"

"It works with Declan."

"Without me trying."

"Which means he's the key to everything."

"I don't get it."

"He can unlock you."

Thinking about what had happened between them after he'd brought her home, she said, "Um…he already has."

Minny's eyebrows shot up again and she snorted. "I meant in a psychic way."

"So did I!"

"Okay, keep your cool. Let's start over. You see visions when you touch Declan."

"Yes."

"Sexual visions."

"Yes."

"Anything else?"

"No."

So what were these visions exactly? Projections into the future? Declan's thoughts? Or her own fantasies? That was part of the problem, always had been—her not being able to distinguish what would happen in the future from what she wished would happen.

"Have you actually fulfilled the visions you've had?" Minny asked.

"Some." Frustrated, Grace said, "I need to be able to use the damn gift with others, like, now!" Thinking about the past, she said, "And it needs to be accurate this time, to show me what I need to know."

"All right. Calm down."

Minny reached over and covered one of Grace's hands with her own. She closed her eyes for a moment, her expression one of deep concentration. Grace felt a little thrill shoot through her. When her cousin blinked her eyes open, her expression cleared.

"Your ability is wrapped up in emotional responses. The reason you can't use it is that you're an emotional mess because you lost trust in a boy who meant a lot to you."

"Tell me something I don't know."

Minny ignored her impatient tone. "You do trust Declan, right?"

"I *want* to trust him." More than any man she'd ever met.

"Good. Then try to be free with him."

"Minny, I've been pretty free."

"Again, I don't mean sexually. When you touch Declan, you're recognizing sexual energy, but not anything else. So use it and turn it around. Simply channel that sexual energy to recognize nonsexual emotions and truths and future events."

Simply...right...

"Let me get this straight. While I'm having racy thoughts about one man, I can see the truth about another?"

"No, of course not. I'm suggesting you open yourself fully to Declan *first*," Minny clarified. "Think of it as practice. Clearing out the cobwebs and all that. One step at a time. If you can trust enough to open up your mind to one man, opening it to others will follow."

Opening her mind to one man was a lot more complicated than it sounded. Grace had done that once and humiliation had been her reward. She didn't trust men. Never had, not since that fateful day that had changed her. More than a dozen years had passed and still she wasn't over it. But she really did want to trust Declan McKenna, and truth be told, there was no reason why she shouldn't.

Could she do it, then? she wondered. Could she handle an ability that had been too much for her when she'd been young and innocent? And trusting...

Her pulse fluttered. "Let's just say this works. How can I distinguish something that will happen from something I'm simply projecting? Or, say, whatever the person's thinking about at that given moment? You can't hold someone to a daydream."

"This isn't an exact science, Grace. Probably most stuff you'll connect with is the day-to-day garbage that goes through all our heads. That's how I reel my customers in, because I can get the vibe of the moment. But if you concentrate…*really concentrate,* you'll get those flashes into the future that the other person doesn't even know about. You may already be getting that with Declan in one area. Now explore the others."

"If I can…"

"You have to be open, to give yourself a chance to figure it all out. Lucky you, having a man like that to help you experiment."

Yeah, lucky her, Grace thought.

The very idea terrified her.

Chapter Nine

Grace was still pretty terrified thinking about resurrecting her psychic ability when a knock at the door made her start. Even knowing Declan was due to come by that evening, she hesitated for a moment, until he identified himself.

The moment she opened the door to let him in, the weight of the world on her shoulders grew a little lighter. Her pulse threaded unevenly. He made her feel not so alone in a horrible situation.

The intense way he was looking at her made her toes curl.

"You look like you could use some grub."

Grace didn't argue. She was starving. When he took her hand, she wasn't ready for him. He sent live voltage shooting through her.

She crawls on the bed on hands and knees with him right behind her. Before she can flip onto her back, he covers her and nudges her thighs open. Shuddering, she lets him in, gasps as he fills her, then moves in her in a rhythm that sends her heart drumming against her ribs.

"Are you okay?"

Declan's words jerked her back to the present.

"Yeah. Sure."

What else would she say—that she'd just had a hot vision with him standing there?

She'd tried to read various people since leaving Minny that morning, but so far her psychic connection remained unconnected with anyone but Declan. Hopefully her cousin had been correct about him being the key to unlocking her.

"Before I forget," she said, "let me get that list of people who work in the Orleans Exchange building for you. I started the list with the names I knew, then stopped by to add anyone I didn't know from the directory."

She went to the counter where she picked up a sheet of paper that she held out to him. He took the list from her, folded it and slipped it into a pocket as she stuffed her wallet and her keys in her pants pockets.

"I'll run checks on everyone on the list by tomorrow," he said.

"Good."

They slipped out to a creole café Grace frequented over on nearby Frenchmen Street. Removed from the glitzy neon lights and blaring music of Bourbon

Street, Frenchmen Street was a two-block-long entertainment district where the locals hung out.

They ordered po'boys and beers. Despite her anxiety, Grace felt herself relax in Declan's company. The small café was dark, intimate. Jazz played low in the background, the musicians wringing the souls out of their instruments. A handful of people were scattered around the place. It would fill up later, but the café was too low-key for tourists searching for the "real" New Orleans.

Grace waited until the waitress took their order and left their table before asking, "So what were you able to do on a Sunday?"

"I'm in the process of tracking down the e-mail the blackmailer sent."

"In the process...what does that involve exactly?"

"Putting my cousin Kevin on the case."

"Your cousin?" She tightened up again and pulled her hand free. "Is he part of the agency?"

"No, but he has no clue as to why I want the information—he only knows I want to find the person who sent a message. Kevin is a programmer and knows a lot of people in the computer industry. I gave him the name of the real ISP and it turns out he has a contact there. He'll see if he can sweet-talk her into giving up some information."

His explanation of what Kevin was looking for left her baffled. She'd never been a techie. She'd never even bought a smart phone. A simple cell phone and a basic computer at home were more than enough for her to handle.

"You think it'll work?" she asked.

"Fingers crossed that Kevin will have the information we need tomorrow."

"Let's hope he can get something that will help."

"At least the address of the computer that sent the message out."

The food and beer arrived. Starving, Grace dug in, took a big bite of her oyster po'boy and washed it down with some beer. Her stomach thanked her. In New Orleans, even the dives had good food.

Waiting until she'd polished off half her sandwich, Grace then asked, "What about the fingerprints?"

"Tomorrow. If we're lucky. If it was put in line with all the other requests, getting results could take months, but my partner, Ian, hit up one of his contacts to get it done fast. And again, your name wasn't mentioned," he assured her. "There was only one set of fingerprints other than yours on the paper. If we nail them, we nail the blackmailer. I also started researching suspects, mostly using the Internet, but by making a call to several contacts, as well."

"And you learned…?"

"It seems Helen Emerson really is Mrs. Clean."

"And Laroche?"

"He was accused of being involved in a Ponzi scheme with some bankers a couple of years ago, but no charges were ever brought against him."

So her instincts about Laroche had been right. "If it's true, though, that means he'd do anything for money."

"*If* it's true. Couldn't find anything on Max Babin. She seems pretty straight up. Raphael Duhon is another story."

"Raphael?" Grace suddenly lost her appetite. "Oh, no. How bad?"

"Years ago he made some bad decisions and posed for suggestive pictures. He was nineteen at the time. I couldn't find anything else since then."

But Raphael was acquainted with the world of adult material and how easily it was distributed. Grace pushed her plate away, but finished her beer in one long gulp.

"So Laroche…or Raphael…"

"Maybe. But let's not jump to conclusions. Let me check out the other people on that list you gave me."

"Of course." Grace didn't want it to be Raphael. She didn't want everything positive in her life to end.

"So how did you spend your day?"

"Visiting relatives. This morning was our monthly brunch together—Mama and Corbett and me."

"Get anything new talking to them?"

Grace shook her head.

"That leaves you the rest of the day. You weren't doing anything dangerous, were you?"

"Dangerous?"

"Trying out your ability on suspects?"

"No…not yet." Grace sighed. "I tried a couple of times with people I ran into on the street." She shook her head. "Nothing. But I've been thinking about it. Assuming I could control the ability, I might get something of value. And then again, I might not… and disrupting my life would be for nothing."

"Not to mention you could put your life in danger. Which brings me back to my question about what we do when we identify the blackmailer."

She'd been thinking about that, too, so she didn't even hesitate. "We steal the photographs—or the files—back."

Declan locked gazes with her as if he were trying to read her. "You're serious."

"Absolutely." Not that she'd ever stolen anything before. Or committed any kind of crime. She was trying to stop a crime from being committed against her family. "Why not?"

"Again, that would be dangerous. You could be caught."

"That's a chance I'll have to take!"

"I think you should just leave things to me."

Grace clenched her jaw. Declan suddenly

reminded her of others who thought she should do as they said. "Don't try to control me."

"I'm trying to help," he said reasonably. "That's why I'm going to ask you to be extra careful."

His expression was reasonable, but something about the glint in his eyes put Grace on edge. She didn't have to be psychic to realize he was holding something back.

"What are you not telling me?"

He raised an eyebrow and for a moment she thought he was going to pretend like he didn't know what she was talking about.

To her shock, he said, "Someone was watching us last night."

"When? At the party? Why didn't you say anything? Point out the person."

"Not at the party, at your place, when we were… together."

Heat flooded her cheeks. "You mean when we—"

"Exactly. I didn't know anyone was out there until I left to go home. Which I never did, by the way, until you went to the Garden District this morning."

"Wait! You followed me?"

"For your protection in case the guy came back. That's part of my job to see that you're safe."

He ran his knuckles lightly over her cheek and almost caused a vision. But the horror Grace felt at someone watching them precluded anything psychic. And had the person only been watching?

"What if the bastard had another camera?" she asked.

"If he did, I couldn't tell. At that distance, he'd need a telephoto lens to get anything up close and personal. Can't hide something bulky so easily, so no, I don't think so."

"This person watching us..." She could hardly talk about the newest twist in her life. "What did he look like?"

"I wish I could tell you. He was wearing baggy, dark clothing and a cap that hid his face. I chased him into the Quarter and he lost me on Bourbon Street."

That sounded like the guy who'd followed her the night before. "I don't get it," she said. "Back up a minute. How did you know he was watching us in the first place?"

"I sensed it. I could feel the anger he was generating. When you came out on the balcony, his emotions only got stronger. More negative."

"Whoa!" she said. "What am I missing here? You *sensed* it?"

He locked gazes with her for a moment before finally saying, "You're not the only one who inherited a gift. The McKennas in my family all have some psychic ability."

"So you can read my mind?" she choked out, embarrassment searing her. Did that mean he knew the exact nature of her visions?

"I'm an empath," Declan said. "I couldn't tell you what someone was thinking, but I *could* tell you what that person was feeling. Trust me, that guy's feelings were all bad and generated at you."

Trust him? Was that even possible now?

"Why didn't you tell me about your having this ability before?"

"You weren't exactly open to being psychic yourself. I figured if I told you…"

"I might not trust you."

He'd been between a rock and a hard place. Right? Why didn't the realization make her feel better? She'd always had trust issues with men, probably the reason one never took with her. The reason she'd never allowed herself to fall in love.

As she'd told Minny, she wanted to trust Declan, but she just didn't know if she could.

And until she made up her mind about Declan McKenna—until she could trust him fully—she couldn't do as Minny suggested and use him to recharge her psychic power.

ARRIVING AT HIS OFFICE to start running security checks on the people on Grace's list, Declan parked in front of the place. He was still thinking about how Grace had withdrawn once he'd admitted he was psychic.

Which made him wonder why she was so damn negative about the issue.

Most of the McKennas in his family accepted their abilities, but some didn't use them or talk about them or tell anyone about them. They wanted to be like everyone else.

Only, no matter that she said that's what she wanted, Grace Broussard didn't want to be like everyone else.

He sensed she took pride in being her own person, so why the prejudice against something that would make her stand out more? Even if she was thinking of using her gift to test the suspects, he sensed how badly she didn't want to.

How conflicted she was.

What kind of humiliation had she suffered?

The moment he unlocked the outside door, he realized he wasn't alone. A light came from his cousin's office.

"Ian?" he called out as he entered.

"In here."

Declan stopped in the doorway. "What are you doing here on a Sunday night?"

"I had nothing better to do, so I thought I would stop by and do some paperwork. You?"

"Grace gave me a list of people who work in the Orleans Exchange building. I figured I might as well start running the security checks."

"If you want help with that…"

"Sure. I'll make a copy of the list and we can divide it. Maybe I'll get to bed at a decent hour tonight."

Making a copy only took a minute. He drew a line, dividing the top half for him, the bottom half for his cousin. As he handed the copy to Ian, Declan brought him up to speed on all that had happened since they'd spoken the day before.

"Whew!" Ian said, glancing at the names on the list. "Your case is escalating fast."

"And we have a little more than forty-eight hours to resolve it or Grace's reputation will have a permanent stain." And her heart would be broken—Declan couldn't stand the thought of that happening. It would change Grace, he knew it. "Not to mention the careers of her mother and brother may very well be ruined."

"When you figure out who's doing this…what then?"

"Grace wants to retrieve the photographs."

Ian started. "Serious?"

"So she claims."

"Might work."

"If the bastard hasn't distributed copies everywhere." A very likely possibility.

"How do you feel about doing something not exactly legal?"

"I'm just working the case the best I can for the client," he muttered.

Declan knew Ian was referring to his background as a lawman. He'd known guys on the job who'd done things that hadn't been strictly legal to make a case. He'd never done so himself, but he'd looked the other way a few times.

There was no looking away with Grace and her family at stake. She was trying to save them all without telling anyone but him. He and Ian were the only ones who knew what she was going through. And *he* was the only one who knew how torn up she was inside about the situation.

He couldn't—*wouldn't*—let her down.

With the list next to him, Ian started tapping away at his keyboard. "The client won't budge on going to the authorities?"

"Not an inch. And I'm afraid Grace is going to put herself in danger by doing something she shouldn't. She's determined that we find the guilty party and…she has the gift," Declan admitted.

"Aha." Ian murmured, looking up from his computer screen. "Now isn't that a coincidence, the both of you having the gift."

Noting the vibrant tone in his cousin's voice, Declan asked, "What does that have to do with anything?"

"The prophecy."

"I don't get it."

"If you're both psychic—perhaps together you can overcome the danger."

"Wait a minute, Ian. I thought you didn't believe in the prophecy."

"I don't. But *you* do."

"It doesn't matter anyway. Grace is a client."

"One who concerns you. Personally."

"Because she's gotten a raw deal and I want to help her."

"And that's all?"

That's all Declan would admit to.

Chapter Ten

Not wanting anyone to be able to get into her apartment, Grace made sure all her windows and French doors were securely locked. After racing upstairs, she'd gone out on the balcony and had watched Declan as he'd searched the area around her building. Apparently no one or nothing alerted him, because he'd quickly left.

Still, that didn't mean her blackmailer couldn't come back for her. What would he have done the night before if Declan hadn't chased him off? Would he have tried to break in? Or did he just like watching?

Shivering at the thought, she pulled all her curtains and blinds as if that could keep her safe. At least it would give her some privacy.

About to undress, she reached into her pants pocket to remove her wallet. Not there. Frowning, she checked her usual dumping place—a table by the door—but it wasn't there, either. Wondering if she could have forgotten removing it when she came in, she checked all the nearby flat surfaces—tables, shelves, counter.

No wallet.

It had to be at the café.

Thinking about it, Grace remembered taking out her wallet to pay for the meal, but Declan had pre-empted her, as if they were on a date rather than having a business meeting. Sitting down at the time, her mind racing over everything he'd told her, she probably hadn't paid enough attention to what she was doing. Apparently she hadn't shoved the wallet back into her pocket securely.

Finding the delivery menu on her kitchen cork board, she called the bar. "This is Grace Broussard—"

"Hey, chér."

Recognizing the bartender's voice, she said, "I was just down there with a friend, Jake. I think I might have dropped my wallet—"

"I'll go look."

Grace held her breath as she waited. She'd had her wallet lifted once and reporting her credit cards stolen and replacing everything inside had been a royal pain. If it wasn't at the café, then she'd more than likely dropped it on the street somewhere. What a nightmare that would be!

"C'mon, c'mon, be there," she whispered.

A moment later, Jake's "Found it under the table" allowed her to breathe easier.

"I'll be right there to get it."

Grabbing her keys, she raced out of the apartment, double-locking the door behind her. Considering the things that had been happening to her, she didn't like going out alone this late. But Declan had swept the place for trouble mere minutes ago and hadn't found anything to raise his hackles. All she had to do was run to the café, get her wallet and run back. That shouldn't take more than ten minutes.

Even so, racing back to Frenchmen Street, she kept her guard up and her head turning and was relieved to make it there without incident.

When she entered the café, the bartender spotted her immediately and pulled her wallet from behind the counter. "Here you go, chér."

"Let me give you something for your trouble." Grace opened her wallet, still intact with money and credit cards and driver's license, thankfully.

"No need." Jake waved her off. "We want good customers to be happy. You can give a big tip to whoever waits on you next time you come in."

"Thanks, then."

She stuffed the wallet securely in her pocket and took off. Walking fast, she slowed when she came to the corner and got a quick flash of a shadow melding into a doorway she would have to pass to get home.

Her pulse charging, Grace was glued to the spot. Had she really seen something or was her imagination simply engaged after what Declan had told her?

Instinct told her not to pass that doorway....

Keeping her head cocked slightly so she could see from the corner of her eye, she crossed the street. Before her foot hit the curb, movement from the doorway had her on the run, away from danger.

Away from home.

Away from people.

Except for him.

The slap-slap of his shoes behind her drove her forward faster. One block. Two. She threw a fast glance over her shoulder. The dark-clothed stalker was still behind her, his hands stuck in his pockets, his shoulders hunched as he power-walked after her. Wearing a cap that hid his face, he fit Declan's description of the man who'd been outside her apartment the night before.

Small apartment buildings and shotgun houses gave way to storage buildings and half-empty parking lots that serviced the French Market. She darted into the closest lot looking for somewhere, anywhere to hide. Someone, anyone to help her as had the couple two nights before.

But tonight she was alone. On her own. No buildings or bushes or anything but a few cars and more trucks.

Flashing a look over her shoulder, she confirmed her stalker was just outside the fencing. He would see her in a minute. Her mind raced for a way out of this.

Then her mouth went dry and her stomach knotted as instinct took over and she dived under a truck to save herself. Rolling to her back, she flattened her body and inched under the middle of the vehicle.

Don't let him find me…don't let him find me…

The words choked her mind even as she heard footsteps nearby.

The person stopped, as if looking around for something…*for her*…and then came directly toward her.

Terror gripped Grace, tightened her chest. What to do? If he found her and ducked down under the truck to get to her, she would roll away and run again. Run where?

Think…think!

Back to Frenchmen Street. It wasn't that far. She could make it…she didn't have a choice.

Again, the feet stopped. Closer this time. She could see them now. Dark shoes, dark pants. He was close enough to hear her so she nearly stopped breathing. She silently sucked in a small amount of air, then slowly let it ease back out again.

The man moved off in another direction and Grace thought she could cry in relief. She would wait a minute, make sure he was still going off away from her, then slip out from the truck and hightail it to Frenchmen Street.

Just then her cell phone pierced the quiet!

Grace thought surely her heart would explode with her panic. Pulling the cell from her pocket, she fumbled with suddenly stiff fingers to shut it off.

"Who's there?" came a male voice.

Making Grace scramble in the opposite direction. By the time she popped up out from under the truck, he was there, mere feet away, flashing a bright light in her face.

"Security!" the man ground out. "What the hell are you up to?"

Certain this wasn't the same man who'd been stalking her—he was middle-aged and stocky and he wasn't wearing anything on his balding head, Grace looked around wildly.

"Someone was following me. I was trying to hide so he couldn't get to me."

The man swung his flashlight around the parking lot. "Don't see anyone now."

"I swear he's out there."

"I can call the cops."

"No! Please, I just want to go home. A taxi. I need a taxi."

"How far you going?"

"I'm in the Marigny."

"C'mon. I'll take you. My vehicle's over there." He flashed his light on an SUV with a security emblem on the side.

"Are you sure? I don't want to put you to any trouble."

"Hey, I got two daughters of my own. I'd hope someone would help them if they got themselves in trouble."

From his tone, Grace realized he didn't exactly believe her story. He probably thought she'd done something to bring trouble to herself. That was okay. Whatever worked for him. She'd get home safely without having to call the police.

Or Declan.

As they headed for his vehicle, he flashed his light around the lot. "Whoever was following you musta skedaddled."

"Thanks to you."

She'd been looking, too, and hadn't seen anyone.

What if no one really had been following her and, fueled by Declan's telling her about chasing some guy into the French Quarter, her imagination had simply gone ballistic?

They arrived at the SUV. The security guard opened the passenger door for her, then got behind the wheel. Grace gave him her address and they were off.

"You sure you don't want to call someone?" the

security guard asked as he started the vehicle and drove it off the lot. "If not the police, a brother maybe? Or a boyfriend?"

A reminder that her cell had gone off.

Declan?

Grace said, "No, really, I'll be fine. I promise once I get inside, I'll double lock my door and won't open it again until daylight."

Starting to feel foolish, she took a peek at her cell. She had a voice mail. Probably Declan. She'd listen to it once she was inside. In the meantime, she swung her gaze in every direction as they zigzagged the several blocks home. She didn't stop searching the shadows until the SUV stopped in front of her building.

"I'll sit here until you get inside."

"Thanks again."

Grace looked around as she raced to the entry door. Unlocked again. Her pulse raced as she set the latch and then went up the stairs slower than she normally would, her cell in hand in case she *had* to call the police.

Though she was grateful when she safely arrived at her apartment door, Grace cautiously unlocked it and then listened hard. Nothing to alarm her. The lights were still on and everything looked exactly as it had when she'd left to fetch her wallet.

Relieved, she stepped inside and deadbolted the door. After which she threw her wallet and keys on the little table meant for that purpose.

Staring at the cell phone, she wanted to throw it down, too. She thought to leave Declan's message until morning—no doubt he wanted her to call him back, right now, which probably she should.

How she longed for some downtime, a few hours in which she didn't have to think about anything disturbing.

If she didn't get back to Declan, though, she knew he would start worrying that something had happened to her. It was a kind of caring that went beyond their business deal, no doubt due to the fact that they'd slept together. Even if that had been a mistake, it had changed the way she looked at him, thought of him. No doubt it affected him, too. They were bound together by more than a contract.

The reason she'd jumped on him when she'd learned he hadn't told her about being psychic.

She connected to her voice mail.

The voice on the recorded message was not Declan's, nor any she recognized.

The whisper was low and sexless.

And threatening.

"That was a sample of what your life will be like if you don't get the money…"

"YOU HAVE TWO CHOICES," Declan told Grace after listening to the message she'd saved for him to hear. She'd called to tell him what happened after he left. Luckily no traffic cop had been around looking to hand out speeding tickets—he'd gotten back to her place in record time. "Either we go to the authorities, or you move in with me until this is over."

"I'm not going to the authorities."

"All right. How soon can you get your things together?"

"I'm not going to let this pervert drive me out of my home, either!"

Declan clenched his jaw tight. Grace was too stubborn for her own good. If that creep had caught up to her and something had happened to her...

"All right," he conceded. "Then I'll move in with you."

"You're my employee!"

Indeed, he was. Declan had to keep reminding himself of that. Hard to do when he'd slept with the woman who'd hired him. Not only did he want to hold her in his arms again, he wanted above all things to keep her safe.

No matter what he'd told his cousin—what he would tell her—that feeling went beyond the job.

"A *good* employee," he emphasized. "That's what I'm trying to be. You need protection, so think of me as your personal bodyguard."

"That's not what I hired you to do. Besides, if I have a bodyguard following me around, that'll flash a big warning. People will know—"

"Not if you don't tell them. Let them think I'm your…significant other. I'll still be working the case—either together or on my own while you're at work."

A delicate color flooded her cheeks, but she didn't seem able to object.

Declan thought about what it would be like to be Grace's significant other. She was everything he went for in a woman—attractive, smart, strong. Well, mostly strong. She still hadn't dealt with whatever was stopping her from using her gift. And that was okay with him for now—considering the situation, it would probably get her into even more trouble.

He didn't want to think about what Ian had implied, didn't want to think he was falling for the woman.

His heart was elsewhere, right?

He tried to conjure Lila's image and for the first time since leaving New Mexico, but couldn't quite manage it. Instead, he kept seeing Grace—entering his office, at the fund-raiser, in his arms, naked as the day she was born.

She was staring at him now, wide-eyed, as if she could read his mind. Which probably she could if she touched him.

No more touching, he thought.

What if he fell for Grace?

...should they act on their feelings, they will put their loved ones in mortal danger...

The curse...he'd already acted....

It wasn't too late, Declan assured himself. While he was attracted to Grace, liked her, cared about what happened to her, he didn't love her.

So all he had to do was keep himself from falling for her and she would come out of this all right.

At least she would be alive.

Chapter Eleven

First thing Monday morning, Grace headed for Voodoo accompanied by her new roommate. In the end, she'd let Declan stay the night. On the sofa. She still hadn't wrapped her mind around the whole body-guard thing, but she did feel safe in his company. At least physically. Emotionally was another story. If only he'd told her about being psychic from the start.

"So let me know when you're ready to leave," Declan said, maintaining a slight distance from her as he'd been doing all morning. "I can be here in five minutes."

She checked her watch—she was running a few minutes behind. Having added some last-minute designs to his new collection, Raphael was anxious to see how they fit her so the seamstress could alter the garments the way he wanted them changed. Considering the kind of mood he'd been in lately, Grace didn't want to keep him waiting.

"I have to run," she said. "Don't worry, I'll be tied

up all day. If you don't hear from me otherwise, pick me up at five."

Declan nodded. "Will do. Hopefully, I'll have something useful by the end of the day."

With that, she hurried into the Orleans Exchange Building, walking blindly past the security station before she was stopped by a singsong "Morning, Miss Grace."

"Eula. Hey."

"You okay?"

Grace realized the security guard was staring at her with a concerned expression. "Just in a hurry."

"I thought maybe something was troubling you."

She gave Eula a forced smile and headed straight up the stairs to the Voodoo offices. Raphael was talking to the receptionist. When she entered, he whirled around and a smile lit his face.

"Ah, Grace, there you are! Good news. The New Orleans *Rising Sun* is going to do a color spread on Voodoo in next Sunday's edition."

"Terrific."

"The editor set up separate interviews for us," Raphael said.

"Us?"

"Yes, of course. He's assigned a reporter to interview you at home. This evening, at six-thirty. You don't have a problem with that, do you?"

As much as she would like to get out of it, Grace

knew she needed to do this for the sake of the business. "No, of course not."

"Good. Because I already gave the editor your address."

Someone was coming to her home? That put Grace on edge. "Why at my apartment rather than here?"

"I imagine the reporter wants to see how Voodoo Woman lives," Raphael said.

That's what concerned her. Grace didn't like it, not considering what was going on her life, but she didn't see how she could object. "Fine. I'll be home, then."

"The new designs are already waiting for you."

"That's why I'm here." Grace headed for the fitting room.

Now uncomfortable after finding the studio dressing room rigged with a camera, she closely inspected her surroundings for any place one could be hidden. And when she didn't find one, she modestly slipped out of what she was wearing and into the first garment.

Beaded and sequin-trimmed, the calf-length aqua gown seemed spun of gossamer. She stepped out into the fitting area, but Raphael and Magda were nowhere in sight. Though it was designed with its own stretchy fitted slip that clung to her curves like glue, Grace imagined she simply looked nude beneath the delicate material.

She was frowning at herself in the full-length

mirror when Raphael came up behind her and frowned, as well.

"You do not like Raphael's design?"

She whipped around to find the designer behind her. "It's not that."

"Then what is it?"

"I just feel so…well, naked."

The designer smiled. "Exactly."

Though Grace smiled, too, she couldn't pull off sincerity. "I'm not sure it's…well, appropriate."

Good heavens—had she really become her mother?

Raphael's smile died. "Not appropriate? Have the aliens replaced my fearless Grace with a clone?"

Realizing she was reacting to the blackmail, that she never would have been bothered by the garment if her sexuality hadn't been put on notice, Grace said, "I guess I'm not really myself today."

Raphael sighed. "It happens." He spread his hands and pouted, mocking her. "Are we done with our hissy fit?"

Grace stared at Raphael and saw not the man who'd given her a chance to bloom, but someone who was trying to control her rather than treat her as he normally did—like a partner helping to grow his business.

What in the world had happened to him?

Or had he been like this all along and she hadn't seen it?

"Yes, we are done." Grace whirled on her heel and headed for the changing area.

"But the fitting…" Raphael called after her. "We are not through here!"

"For *this morning* we are through!"

At the moment, Grace couldn't think about the consequences. Of course she would care if she lost the job she loved so much, but she couldn't help it. Her nerves were on edge and if she wasn't careful, she might shatter. She had to get out of there. Had to go in search of her self-confidence. Two days ago, she wouldn't have hesitated wearing the gown. But now she was doubting herself and didn't know how she was ever going to get back what the black-mailer had stolen from her.

As she changed into her street clothes, she thought about calling her brother and asking him for a loan. She didn't have to tell him what it was for, right? Sure. He would give her half a mil, no questions asked. Forget that. Besides, Declan had made a good point that the blackmailer could come back for more. That or copies of the photos would undoubtedly still be in someone else's hands.

The only thing for it, then, was to discover the blackmailer's identity and work from there—do whatever it took to get her hands on all copies of the photos.

To her chagrin, she could think of only one way.

Grace changed quickly and headed toward the reception area, expecting Raphael to stop her at any moment. Already regretting her burst of uncharacteristic pique, she still felt she'd been justified.

She stopped at the receptionist's desk. "Laurie, tell Raphael I'll be back to finish the fitting after lunch."

"Will do. Maybe the news will blow off the storm clouds that accompanied him out the door after your fight."

"He told you?"

"I heard. Everyone did. We all gave you a little cheer. He's been impossible lately, hasn't he?"

"I thought it was just me. Any idea why?"

She shrugged. "The word is that his other ventures are suffering. I'm sure his mood is nothing personal. He's just stressed over money."

He wasn't the only one.

That didn't mean he was the blackmailer, Grace told herself. And considering Laurie had known him longer than most of the employees, Grace felt a bit better at the receptionist's evaluation of the situation.

"I'm just going out to get some air. And food. I'll be back in a couple of hours."

"I'll tell him."

Freeing herself of the building lightened her spirit. The endorphins from exercise had always made her feel better. It occurred to her that Declan would expect her to call him, to let him know she was leaving the building. But she needed some time alone, and it was daylight. Hordes of people wandered through the French Quarter, so she would be safe. She power-walked along Decatur, for once not stopping to take in the sights or smells.

Determined to read someone by touch, her pulse quickened. She didn't want to have to depend on using Declan to reinstate her ability, no matter what Minny said.

Her inability to control what she owned rankled. She'd put her gift to sleep and she needed to awaken it, even if meant trying with dozens—or hundreds—of people. And where better to do it than at the French Market. Specifically, the open-air Community Flea Market.

The place was already overcrowded. People bought fruits and vegetables, freshly ground coffee and spices. They sorted through tables of clothing, pored over souvenir tables of Mardi Gras masks and inspected glass perfume bottles. At a table laid out with locally made jewelry, several women huddled together and pawed through display boxes of earrings and necklaces and bracelets.

Grace huddled, too, pressing her shoulder up against the teenager next to her for a moment, as she picked up a bracelet and thoroughly inspected it. Though she concentrated on the girl, tried to see her in a situation away from the market, Grace didn't get a thing off her.

A little way down the aisle, she came to a book stall and reached for the same book as did an older man. Their hands connected. Briefly. Nothing there, either.

Making her way to a fruit stand, she bought a plum and a peach for lunch. She made sure to brush hands with the woman who gave her change…but no glimpse into the future.

Now what? Perhaps the touches were too short-lived. She needed longer to get her focus.

A particularly crowded aisle that afforded no room to get through perfectly suited her purpose.

Touching a man's arm, she murmured, "Excuse me" so low he didn't hear. Which meant she got to touch him longer. She concentrated hard. Harder. A quick blip showed her a reading room, a personal library, but just as she tried to latch on to the vision, it slipped away from her. It was a full minute before he realized she was there.

"Oh, sorry," he said, moving aside.

"No problem," Grace lied, trying not to be discouraged.

She'd had enough time, but couldn't focus enough to latch onto the vision.

Refusing to give up so quickly, she continued her search for someone she could read. It didn't seem to matter who she tried—male or female, young or old—and it didn't seem to matter how long she tried; she barely connected before the connection was severed.

She was simply wasting her time.

HALFWAY THROUGH THE AFTERNOON, Declan entered the Orleans Exchange building in search of Grace. He started up the stairs only to hear raised voices at the top.

"I don't want to see him around here again, do you understand me?"

"But, Mr. Raphael—"

"I'm serious, Eula. If you let your brother in here again, that's it. You're out. Are we clear?"

"Clear," the security guard muttered.

Eula wasn't looking too happy by the time she came into Declan's view. Neither was Raphael.

"Why you ever thought it was all right to give him free rein around here…"

The designer was red-faced as he whipped by Declan with barely a nod, making Declan wonder what Eula's brother had done to be banned from the building.

"Afternoon, Eula. I'm looking for Grace."

"Miss Grace is in the offices." Eula gave a dark look to where Raphael had disappeared. "You go right on in."

"Thanks."

Considering the security guard tended to give him a suspicious glare and a hard time, Declan was surprised. Then, perhaps Eula was so angry at Raphael that she was giving him a break for once. He took it before she could change her mind and entered the designer's offices.

The name plate at the end of the front desk identified the receptionist as Laurie Hanson. "May I help you?"

"I'm here for Grace."

"Grace? She's still in the fitting room. Apparently one of the dresses didn't hang right, so Raphael and Magda are working on it."

"No problem. I wasn't supposed to meet her for another hour." He pulled his forehead into a purposeful frown.

"What is it? Maybe I can help."

"I'm waiting for an important e-mail and I managed to forget my iPhone. I thought maybe…"

"I can let you use my computer for a minute."

Declan smiled at her cooperation. "It may take more than a minute. Is there another computer… maybe one that's free?"

"Oh, sure. There must be. Just about everyone here has one."

Great. Just what he didn't want to hear. Lots of computers meant lots of possible terminals the blackmailer could have used. Then again, logic was they were networked and information coming from this location could be accessed by any one of the computers. He hoped.

Declan followed the receptionist, sweeping his gaze around what looked like a showroom—no computer here—and then a workroom with long tables filled with bolts of brilliantly colored cloth and boxes of sparkly trims. A couple of seamstresses worked at sewing machines at the windows.

"It's late in the day so most of the office staff is already gone," Laurie confided.

Indeed, three offices sat to one side of the workroom—all with computers, but all seemingly locked.

The receptionist turned a corner. "Here you go. I figured this one would be free."

Declan looked into what must be a break room. A computer in the corner hummed in welcome.

He smiled at the receptionist. "Thanks, Laurie. It may take a while. If Grace finishes before I do, would you let her know I'm back here?"

"Sure thing. Take your time."

Indeed, he would. Sitting before the terminal, he jiggled the mouse to wake up the monitor. Delving into Control Panel and then Network Connections, he scanned the information. According to Kevin, each computer on the network would have a unique identifier that would allow someone to tell which specific computer the e-mail was sent from. The IP address on this computer didn't match the one Kevin gave him, but he took down the information in case he needed it later.

Not wanting to be caught, Declan walked to the door and poked his head out to make sure no one was headed his way. All clear.

Kevin had told him a business system would have both a public and private network. The public network had access to the Internet, while the private network contained the company's computers. When the router received requests from the computers on the private network, it forwarded them to the Internet via the public network.

Back at the computer, Declan delved into Documents and Settings and traced his way to the profiles of the users and copied the mail folders to his flash drive. If the e-mail came from one of the Voodoo computers, he had no compunction about using the flash drive to nail the offending e-mail to the correct profile.

When the transfer was complete, he left the computer and moved down the corridor. Spotting an empty office with a computer, he quickly accessed the IP—not a match—and copied it. He was able to get to two more computers with the wrong IP addresses before he heard voices. People were approaching. He got out of there and back to the reception area.

Smiling at the receptionist, he said, "Thanks, Laurie. I appreciate the help."

"Did you get what you needed?"

"I hope so."

Declan's gut tightened as he thought about what Grace must be going through, while still maintaining her poise and work ethic. He appreciated that about her. He appreciated so many things. He would do anything to help her—as proven by his messing around with Voodoo's computers—to see a smile of relief on that beautiful face.

If anyone were to hurt Grace…

Declan told himself to settle down and rid his head of all personal thoughts. He couldn't allow himself to get sucked in any deeper, couldn't let himself fall for Grace. He had to stick to the investigator-client relationship for her sake.

He was still trying to get his head in order when she came out of the fitting area. One look at her jolted him through and through.

He wanted to wrap a possessive arm around her waist…wanted to kiss her…

When he got to his feet, it took all his willpower to keep his distance.

"Ready to go?" he asked.

"I'm finished here."

He followed Grace out to the street and looked around for a taxi. Too much to expect to find one at rush hour. They walked to the nearest stop for the Riverfront streetcar that would take them along the Mississippi to Esplanade.

"The *Rising Sun* is doing a feature on Raphael and his designs for next Sunday's issue," Grace told him after they boarded the rush-hour-crowded car. "You know, local boy does good and all that. Well, apparently, they think I'm part of Voodoo's success."

"You are, of course. A major part. But still," he went on, worried about the timing. Would a reporter see through her thin skin and use it to his advantage? He lowered his voice and dropped his head so he was practically whispering in her ear. "Agreeing to do an interview right now…do you think that's wise considering the circumstances?"

Grace sighed. "I don't like it, either. I didn't arrange it, Declan. I didn't even know about anyone wanting to talk to me until I walked in today. Maybe with you there, it'll be okay. I kind of walked out on Raphael this morning, so I can't cancel. He assured me it would only take half an hour. The reporter will be at my place at six-thirty."

"Walked out on him? Walked where?"

"Just out for some air. Okay, the French Market."

"You walked all that way alone?"

"I do that a lot since it's on the way home."

"You know what I mean. I asked you to let me know when you were leaving."

"I didn't know until I did it, okay? And I'm fine, so let's drop it."

Grace had an edge to her that didn't bode well. She was too jumpy and Declan feared she was bound to make mistakes, to give the reporter some opening she didn't want.

Chapter Twelve

Declan volunteered to stop at a local bar and get some takeaway so Grace could go straight to the apartment and freshen up before the reporter arrived. As she approached her building, she noted the woman waiting outside the doorway and recognized her immediately.

Jill Westerfield—what was *she* doing here? Something about Corbett?

A bit anxious, Grace asked, "Excuse me, but are you looking for me?"

"I certainly am, Ms. Broussard." The blonde held out her hand. "Jill Westerfield. I'm doing the piece on you for the New Orleans *Rising Sun*."

"I didn't expect you until later."

Taking the woman's hand, Grace did her best to get something off her, but as had happened to her all day, she got a blip—*Jill at her computer, undoubtedly writing this story*—and then nothing, making her feel as if she were right on the edge of a breakthrough and then blocked.

As she led the way, Grace's mind whirled. What relationship did the reporter have to Larry Laroche? Or to her brother for that matter? As she unlocked the apartment door, she vowed she would answer every question carefully, not give the reporter an opening she would regret later.

Once inside, Grace asked, "Can I offer you something to drink?"

"No, thanks." The Westerfield woman had already wandered into Grace's living room and was giving the furnishings and artwork a critical once-over. "Eclectic taste."

"Make yourself comfortable, Ms. Westerfield."

Grace took the leopard-print chaise. The reporter sat on the sofa and pulled out a small recorder, which she set on the table between them.

"I always record my interviews."

Now why did being recorded make her pulse rush? Grace wondered. She could handle an interview, for heaven's sake. Maybe her hesitancy came from the recorder itself, which reminded her of the camera....

"Shall we begin?"

The interview began with all the questions Grace had expected.

How had Raphael found her?

What kind of a working relationship did they have?

Did he design with her specifically in mind?

And then the focus turned to Grace personally.

"How does it feel to be recognized as Voodoo Woman when you're out in public?"

"I'm not, actually. Not unless I'm at a gathering where I'm modeling some of Raphael's designs as part of my job as his spokesperson."

"No one recognizes you?"

"Well, if they do, they're very polite and leave me my privacy." Which was more than the reporter was wont to do, she was certain.

Just then, the front door opened and Declan walked in with a large bag of luscious-smelling food that he set on the breakfast bar.

Realizing the reporter's interest was piqued, Grace said, "This is Declan McKenna. Declan, this is Jill Westerfield with the *Rising Sun.*"

"Mr. McKenna."

"Ms. Westerfield." Declan shook her hand.

Just then, Declan's cell rang. "I'll take this in the bedroom." He flipped open the phone as he moved off.

Wishing he hadn't been interrupted—she could use his support right now—Grace regrouped.

"I'd like to ask you a series of questions that will help me know you better as a person."

Though her stomach tightened, Grace kept that smile plastered to her lips. "Ask away."

"Describe yourself."

"Curious about the world…a lot of varied interests…a loyal friend…"

"I mean your looks."

Of course she did. The reporter wanted her to say something that would make her look arrogant. Or that would at least raise a few eyebrows.

"Tall…dark-haired…"

"My, you're modest."

"As Mama raised me to be."

"Your mother." The reporter leaned in closer to the recorder. "Assistant District Attorney Sandra Broussard, soon to be *Judge* Broussard if public opinion is to be believed. Let's talk about *her.*"

Though she was seething inside, Grace tilted her head and in her most sugar-coated accent said, "Let's not, Ms. Westerfield. This interview is actually about the brilliant designer who gave me a chance to wear lovely clothing."

"But you're a reflection of his success."

"Yes, I am."

"And A.D.A Broussard had a hand in shaping you."

"Let's be clear on this. This interview is about Voodoo Woman."

Jill stared at her for a moment as if trying to think of a way to get her to reveal something sensational.

Grace took the time to recover her temper. Reporters were always trying to get the goods on a politician, even a clean one. Wait until she told Corbett the object of his affections was another reporter. Or did he already know? Surely he couldn't

be that careless again. Imagining what Jill Westerfield might do with the photograph the blackmailer
had sent, she shuddered inwardly.

"What does your family think of you, Ms.
Broussard?"

"You would have to ask them."

Grace could see the reporter's jaw clench as she
took another good look around the living area. She
was looking for something…anything to put Grace
in an unfavorable light. Grace was certain of it.

"If you were going to change one thing…what
would it be?"

"Nothing," Grace said. "I wouldn't change one
little thing. I like who I am."

"You do seem at ease with yourself."

"Is there something wrong with that?"

"I just wonder how other people view what you
do. How do they feel about your ads. The photographs are…well, suggestive."

Grace had thought she'd been prepared for
anything from the reporter…but not that.

"Ms. Westerfield, the ads may be sensual because
the clothes are, but no more so than advertisements
designed for a great number of products."

"So you are selling sex?"

A sound from the foyer made Grace glance back
to see Declan standing there, watching from a

distance. He was glowering at the reporter. How long had he been there, covering her back?

"Ms. Westerfield," Grace said, not willing to let the reporter continue along this path. "I'm surprised you're doing this article for the *Rising Sun* at all."

"Why is that?"

"Your relationship with Larry Laroche—"

"Larry is just an acquaintance."

Remembering the way Laroche had put a possessive arm around the woman's waist at the fundraiser, Grace doubted that. And it had been the reporter who'd pulled him away from the argument with Helen Emerson.

"You know Larry Laroche is running for city council member against my brother. I assume your editor won't let that influence your article?"

The reporter's spine stiffened. "You've had a long day, Ms. Broussard. I won't take up any more of your time." She stood and snatched up her recorder. "Thank you for your candid responses."

"My pleasure."

THE MOMENT Jill Westerfield was out the door, Declan said, "You handled her well."

Grace seemed boneless now that the reporter was gone, and Declan wanted to put an arm around her for support. Wanted to, but didn't. *Keep this on a business level*, he reminded himself. *Keep Grace safe.*

"I felt like I was set up," she said. "Do you think Laroche arranged this interview?"

"Could be. I don't know that we can prove it."

"Or what good it would do if we could."

He'd tried reading the reporter the moment he walked in the door, but she'd had her emotions locked up tight. The only thing he'd gotten from her coming back into the room after taking the phone call was contempt. Because she had contempt for what Grace did for a living? That didn't bode well for an even-handed article.

Not wanting to worry Grace, he said, "That call I took was from my cousin Kevin."

"And?"

"Let me start at the beginning. While you were busy with your fittings this afternoon, I was doing a little investigating on my own at Voodoo."

Grace started. "Investigating how?"

"I got the IP address off the computer in the break room. And several other computers in the offices, as well."

"IP address?"

"It's something that'll tell us if we have the right computer. The one the blackmailer used. Kevin already confirmed the building address. Now he confirmed the computer as belonging to Voodoo."

"So you're saying Raphael's guilty. Great!"

He could sense how much Grace hated this. Hated that she couldn't trust the man she worked for.

"Laurie told me he's been having some financial difficulties."

"Maybe. None of the computers I checked matched, so it's another computer in the building."

"How are we going to find out for sure?"

"Let's eat before the food gets cold," Declan said. "I could use some brain food."

Grace fetched the plates and flatware, while Declan pulled containers from the bag. He'd bought fried shrimp and pan-fried oysters along with sweet potato fries and coleslaw. Luckily, she had a healthy metabolism. They both heaped their plates with food.

Declan popped a shrimp in his mouth and said, "I wish I'd had more time to figure out Jill Westerfield. She held herself together tightly, yet I got some strange vibes off her. It felt like…contempt."

"She wasn't shy about showing her feelings about what I do for a living."

"Maybe."

They fell silent for a moment as they ate standing at the counter.

Then Grace asked, "What do we do next?"

"We need to get back into the offices, get to any remaining computers. But in the meantime, I pulled user files from the network. We can look through them, see if we get anything of worth."

"What about passwords?"

"Kevin might be able to help with that."

"I hate this."

She didn't have to tell him—Declan could feel how sick this made her.

"The question is—do you hate doing this more than blackmail?"

"I guess not."

They quickly devoured the food before setting up her laptop on the living-room coffee table. There they could view whatever came up together. Declan inserted the flash drive.

"I grabbed all the user files I could find," he explained as the information came up on the monitor. "We just have to figure out who is who."

"Voodoodesigns is obviously Raphael."

"A good place to start."

Declan opened those files and scanned them at random. "All work related. Nothing personal. Of course I can't get into his email. I'll have to leave that to Kevin."

"Pinsandneedles must be Magda," Grace said. "The seamstress."

Her files were a combination of business and personal, but nothing there raised any suspicion. Nor did numbercruncher or slavegirl.

"One left. Baronsamedi," Declan muttered. "What does that stand for?"

"Baron Samedi is one of the loas—sort of a saint, but in the Voodoo religion."

The contents were anything but saintly. They were also inappropriate for the office.

"This isn't professional-looking stuff, but the kind shot by amateurs."

"Or by hidden cameras."

Grace gasped when they came to a file of photos of a naked man. Alone in the shots, he was in the throes of ecstasy. Thinking the shots could have been taken by a hidden camera like the one in the dressing room, she tore her gaze from the computer.

She took a deep breath and met Declan's gaze.

"Could any of the people you work with be associated with black market adult photos?" he asked.

"Not that I know of."

"Is this the loyal employee speaking? Or the psychic?"

"I haven't been able to rouse my psychic ability. I've tried, but as soon as I even start to get the slightest something it disappears in a poof."

"So you *have* been trying."

"Guilty."

Grace could tell Declan didn't like it and was grateful that he kept that opinion to himself.

"What do you think the problem is?" he asked.

"I know what the problem is—trust," she said. "Rather, lack thereof."

"In the people you've been touching?"

"In my ability…in myself."

Declan stared at her a moment before asking, "What in the world happened to you all those years ago to make you feel this way?"

Grace swallowed hard. This wasn't something she shared. Ever. Minny knew about it—the only person she'd ever told—and of course there were those involved. And enough witnesses to have made high school miserable for her.

She didn't know why, but she wanted Declan to understand. And the only way that was going to happen was if she was honest with him at last. He would understand if anyone would. Surely he'd had some issue with his own psychic ability.

"I made a mistake with one of my visions," she finally said. "A big one." Turning, Grace looked straight at her favorite French Quarter acquisition. She hadn't even been shopping when the gilt-edged, peacock-blue trunk had appeared before her saying "buy me." She hadn't been able to resist. "I saw what I wanted to see rather than what was."

She couldn't resist it now.

Rising, she walked to the trunk and knelt before it.

Inside she'd tucked away things that spoke to her with equal resonance. As always admiring the intricate pattern painted on the lid, she raised it to gaze at her memories. The well-worn pink shoes Cousin

Minny had bought her when she was eight sat right on top. A feathered Mardi Gras mask that Grand-mama Madelaine had bought for her lay right next to the shoes. But it was the third item on top—the one out of sync with the others—that always held the most power over her.

She picked up the bra of pink lace and padding—a tactile reminder of why she'd shut down her supposed gift.

"Terrence didn't actually lead me on. I did that to myself." Grace couldn't look at Declan. "I believed the visions in my head, believed in the magic."

"How old were you?"

"Fifteen."

"You were young. That made it easy to make a mistake."

She'd been too naive, had misinterpreted what she'd seen because she had wanted to. She'd gone oh-so-willingly with the boy she'd been crazy about.

"Terrence drew me into the garden away from the party celebrating the end of the school year," Grace told him. "I let him kiss me…touch me…I'd seen it all earlier in a vision, so I knew it was to be. I let him seduce me. I would have lost my virginity to him, but this girl Dusty came along and Terrence backed off and apologized all over the place to her." To his *real* girlfriend. "He told Dusty that he was innocent, that I'd led him astray…"

"I'm sure that was a horrible experience for a fifteen-year-old."

"You have no idea." Humiliated, she'd suffered Dusty's scornful expression. In the dark shadows of the garden, she'd fruitlessly tried to refasten her bra. In the end, she'd let it be. "I ran through the party, heard the laughter of the other kids all the way home. It was a mercy that Mama wasn't waiting up for me."

Had Mama known, she no doubt would have issued one of her edicts about what was and what wasn't acceptable behavior. Grace had always known she was unacceptable in her own family.

"So that's when you stopped using your gift."

"That was it. I totally misinterpreted what I saw— my vision didn't include Dusty interrupting Terrence trying to have sex with me or his telling everyone I seduced him. My humiliation was complete."

In the wee hours of the morning, with her face all swollen from crying, she'd known what she had to do. In a heartbeat, she'd buried her psychic ability in her subconscious until the night she'd met Declan.

Declan…why did he have the power to awaken it?

Maybe because he was a man who accepted her as she was, she thought, replacing the bra and closing the lid on the trunk. Maybe that's why she chose to let go of the locked-up place inside her. The place where she'd hidden her psychic ability along with her softer emotions.

The place where she'd hidden the ability to really care about a man.

Chapter Thirteen

"Minny thinks you're the key," Grace told Declan. "That you can unlock me."

"Unlock you?" Declan echoed, thinking Grace's mind wasn't some Pandora's box like the trunk she'd just opened. He was fuming inside, wanting in the worst way to tear off that bastard Terrence's head for what he'd done to Grace. "How is unlocking you supposed to work?"

How could he undo something that had so obviously devastated an innocent young girl that she'd hidden part of herself for years?

"Through touch—"

"You already told me you can see things when you touch me."

"Erotic things…like I saw what was going to happen between us the other night before it happened."

And from her reactions at times, he was pretty sure the visions hadn't ended. As much as he'd tried, he couldn't stop thinking about that night together, either. Even so, he wasn't going to let it happen again.

"What else have you seen?" he asked.

Grace licked her lips. "I've been controlling the visions. For the most part. But Minnie thinks I can use my connection with you to focus on something other than the sexual. And if I can do that with you, maybe I can figure out how to do it with others. With anyone."

"So let's try," Declan said.

"Okay," Grace said softly.

"What do you need me to do?"

"Just sit there, I guess." She sounded breathless when she added, "And let me touch you as much as I need to for a breakthrough."

The thought of Grace touching him at will made Declan's skin burn. The thought of not being able to touch her in return was even more disturbing. But he sat there as she required and tried to keep his expression as normal as possible when she rose from her spot on the floor, joined him on the couch and slipped her hand in his.

One touch and he was ready to lose control.

His gaze glued to her face, Declan realized Grace was trying to cover what she was feeling. Unable to hide her response to him, she was by turns tentative…courageous…anxious…aroused…

He was certainly the last.

He doubted Grace understood how vividly he

could sense her every emotion as she ran the flat of her hand along his arm. If she did, he doubted she would take him there. As it was, for the first time he read her completely. While she struggled with her task, tried for the right touch, tried to gain back the ability she had neatly put away, he was privy to everything going on inside her.

How he'd underestimated her.

Grace was soft and shy and funny and generous. Something like Lila. But beyond that, Grace was loyal and protective and—no matter that she thought herself a coward—fierce and maybe a little foolhardy.

Exactly the type of woman who could win his heart.

That's why, no matter how much he wanted Grace, he couldn't take her in his arms and make love to her lest he incur the prophecy.

If he did…he feared her life would be forfeit, and he would rather live without her than have her for a while and then have to live knowing he'd brought her to her death.

WHAT WAS WRONG WITH HER? Grace wondered. Why couldn't she do this?

She would just start to make the leap from a sexual vision to something more ordinary…and then she would fall back as helpless as a turtle turned on its back. Uttering a sound of frustration, she gave her head a sharp shake as if that would clear it.

"How's it going?" Declan asked.

"Could be better." She stopped, her hand on his shoulder, and noticed that the color in his face had deepened. "Um…are you okay with this?"

"Better than okay. Do whatever you have to do. I'm yours."

His words made her start. *Yours?* Was that figurative or literal? She feared the answer.

"Concentrate!" she ordered herself.

Having worked her way from his hand to his arm to his shoulder, she now slid her palm down over his collarbone. His flesh quaked beneath hers.

He rolls and brings her with him so she lands on top.

She rocks over him and her breasts brush his face.

There was purpose to this, Grace reminded herself as part of her wanted to jerk free from the vision. Indeed, the moment she became aware, she lost her place, so to speak. Reminding herself that Declan was the key to opening her mind, she slid her hand lower, her palm connecting to his chest.

Closing her eyes, she let go, concentrating only on his heartbeat.

Wearing jeans open at the waist, he stands at her stove making breakfast. Bacon in one pan, potatoes in another and a third awaiting the eggs he's whipping.

She places two plates on the counter and leans in to him, watching him.

Grace started—it was working!

He slides inside with a grunt of satisfaction, then wraps his arms around her middle and nuzzles the back of her neck.

What happened? Her brain had once again flashed straight to an erotic vision. Frantic, she zeroed in on the reality of his heartbeat and shifted again.

She drags him down Royal Street to her favorite antiques shop and points to a side table with gold animals' legs. He rolls his eyes and she hits him. He kisses her and pushes her through the door of the shop.

Could what she was seeing be real? Grace wondered. Did she and Declan have a future together?

Her legs lift to circle his thighs. Declan is panting, and she can tell he's fighting to hold back.

One more time, she thought, fighting frustration. This time she slid her hand up from his chest to explore his face. Somehow she removed her mind from the room and focused beyond the instinctive and on the five accepted senses—vision, hearing, touch, taste, smell—she forced the vision back to a nonsexual direction.

He grins down at her…a loopy grin unlike anything she's seen before…he touches her stomach and then covers her face with kisses. Her heart is so full….

"I think I have it," she said at last. "At least with you."

"What did you see?"

She slid away from him. "Normal stuff. But what if it only works with you?"

"We won't know until you try it on other people."

"I know just the place to go."

NO MATTER HOW SPARSE the crowds in other parts of New Orleans, Bourbon Street was never deserted at night. Grace hadn't been to this part of town in a very long time. When they got out of the taxi, she took it all in. The noise, the people, the souvenir shops.

The street was almost foreign to her, and yet it was so alive with sound and movement and color that Grace felt as if she'd come home.

"So what do you think?" Declan asked.

"Contact time."

They walked side-by-side, careful not to touch. Grace now knew she could read Declan. It was the other people who worried her. Would she be able to recognize a blackmailer when she touched him?

Whomp.

Someone in a hurry knocked into Grace with a quick "Oh, excuse me" and she got a mental image of a steaming bowl of lobster bisque being lifted toward an open mouth.

"Wow, that woman sure is hungry."

A whole crowd of tourists streamed down the street, chattering voices assaulting her with images of drinks, food and sex. On the other hand, one girl was thinking about being in bed and reading a good book.

The problem was all the visions were mixed up together. Sights and sounds she couldn't keep straight. They came in flashes. Or worse, waves. Nothing substantial like the ones she had with Declan.

At least something was coming to her, she thought. Working on keeping them straight came next.

One of the street hawkers held a small group of tourists enthralled. He was an actor pretending to be a street cop and bossing the good-humored tourists around.

Grace stopped at the edge of the crowd, but as the actor did his spiel, others stopped, too, brushing shoulders with her, their minds seeming to meld with hers. Dizzy, she tore from the crowd and leaned against a nearby iron railing on the side street.

Keeping up with her, Declan said, "I assume you're seeing things."

"Are you kidding? I'm on overload," she admitted. "My mind is whirling."

"It'll get easier."

"Without so many people, at least I'll be able to tell who's thinking about what."

"We could try someplace less crowded," he suggested.

"I think I've had enough for tonight."

She would start again in the morning and figure out how to focus on one suspect at a time.

THEY WALKED BACK along Royal Street, the sounds of tourists carousing on Bourbon Street in the distance. Walking close to Grace without touching her, Declan felt the shift inside her. She was different. As if at peace with herself.

"I love that you've taken back the part of yourself that you lost for so long," Declan told her.

"I hear a *but* in there."

"But I hope you won't put yourself at risk."

"The whole point of my regaining my ability was to use it to nail the blackmailer!"

Vigilant as always, Declan kept his head turning, his gaze scanning their surroundings as they walked. If anyone was following Grace tonight, Declan would be sure to spot the bastard.

"I understand why you needed to do this, Grace."

And he didn't think it was just to catch a villain. For too long, she'd been without an important part of herself. No wonder she'd gone from school to school, job to job, trying to find some place where she fit in, when all along, part of her had been missing because she hadn't trusted herself to accept who she really was.

"Then what's the problem?" she asked.

"I just want you to stay safe. We need to do this together." That way, he could protect her.

"You mean use your ability in tandem with mine?"

"That could work, don't you think?"

Though it hadn't been what he'd meant, apparently it was what she needed to hear.

"You have a point," he said as they crossed Esplanade and headed straight for her building.

A few minutes later, they were back in her apartment.

"I'm going to check my e-mail," Declan said. "I still haven't heard from Ian about the fingerprints."

"Sure. Go ahead."

The laptop was still on the table by the sofa. He booted it up and quickly went into his e-mail program only to be disappointed.

"Nothing from Ian. Damn! He was certain we would hear by the end of the day."

He was about to close the computer when Grace stopped him. "I might as well check my e-mail."

Parked next to her on the couch, Declan had to keep himself in tight check. He wanted to take her in his arms and hold her, wanted to lose himself in her sweet scent…

She'd gone through several messages when a new one popped up. Her instant anger and fear rocked him.

"What?"

She gasped, "The blackmailer!" and opened the message.

WILL YOU BE READY TO TRADE TOMORROW NIGHT? IF YOU DON'T THINK I'M SERIOUS, CLICK ON THIS LINK AND THEN TELL ME WHAT YOU THINK.

Hands shaking, Grace clicked on the link. Declan could only stare. There she was in the black bustier for all the World Wide Web to see. And that was the least revealing photo of her. There were nude shots, as well—her dressing and undressing. Declan's mouth went dry—this would destroy Grace.

Her fingers rapidly attacked the keyboard.

How could you do this? I thought all you wanted was money!

"He's got to be out there!" Declan quickly went to the windows and peered out at the street. "Otherwise how would he know you were here? That e-mail arriving just then was awfully convenient."

Though he saw nothing amiss and was too far from the street to sense another presence, Declan was torn between running out and trying to find the creep and staying with Grace to make sure she was all right, both physically and emotionally.

Moving back to her side, he waited, mouth dry, for the reply.

I HAVEN'T LAUNCHED THE SITE YET. THE PAGE IS BURIED. I'M STILL WORKING ON IT. CHECK BACK WITH ME AT MIDNIGHT FOR ANOTHER INSTALLMENT.

A panicky Grace typed:

Wait!

No reply.

"He's gone," Declan said, giving Grace a worried look.

"I'm not even sure money would stop him."

Grace looked as if she were about to cry. "What if he does it?" she asked, her voice shaky. "Puts those damn photos of me on the Internet? Even if we figure out who it is, how can we make that go away before everyone sees it? What the hell am I going to do?"

Declan wished he could tell her.

Unable to help himself, he slid an arm around her back and just held her. She trembled against him and fought for control. Every emotion that flashed through Grace wrapped around his heart and pulled them closer. Her anger and despair slowly morphed to something else. Something more positive. Something that had to do with him. With them.

Pulse ticking, he looked down into her face. Her eyes were wide. Her lips parted. He didn't think— he just kissed her.

The touch of her soft mouth was sweet and tentative, as if they'd never gotten this close before. He gently ran his tongue along her lower lip and then explored deeper. That first night had come from a different place, one that was more about reassurance than deep feelings. Hard to believe things could change so fast. Kissing Grace drew from him things that tore Declan up inside.

For a moment, he bore it. He lost himself in the promise he could never make, never take. For a moment, he forgot himself and lost himself in her.

Grace's suddenly churning emotions set off warning bells. He had to stop before things got out of hand. Ending the kiss, he steeled himself and pulled away from Grace. Her surprised expression morphed to neutral in the blink of an eye.

Quickly rising from the sofa, she said, "We probably should try to get some sleep."

He saw through her pretense. Sensed it, knew she wanted him to convince her otherwise. Something he couldn't do, not if he wanted to keep her safe.

"Good thinking," he said.

Knowing he couldn't let anything else—physical or emotional—happen between them.

Chapter Fourteen

The answer came to Grace sometime in the middle of the night. Though she longed for Declan to share her bed, he slept on the sofa again. That kiss kept her awake for hours, listening for any sound from the next room.

Listening for him.

How could this have happened to her? How could she have fallen in love with the man she'd hired to get her out of trouble?

Perhaps it was because she'd chosen at last to offer her complete trust.

Lying alone and awake, she had too much time to think. And mostly what she thought about other than Declan was her family. They trusted her and to this point she'd betrayed that trust and had kept them in the dark. She couldn't keep the blackmail threats from them any longer. Telling them all wasn't something she wanted to do. She'd hoped to keep this from Mama and Corbett to protect them. And yes, to protect herself from their disapproval.

Now she had no choice.

She didn't have the money to pay the blackmailer, she couldn't find him to take back the photographs, and now her time was running out.

DECLAN WAS UP before her, looking far more rested than she when Grace wandered out of the bedroom, showered and dressed. He had fresh coffee ready and handed her a mug.

"I probably should stay away from caffeine," she said even as she drank. "My nerves are shot. To be honest, Declan, I think it's time I told Mama and Corbett what they might be in for. I thought I would do that first thing this morning."

"Good for you. I'll go with you for backup."

"I need to do this myself, Declan. I need to be honest with my family about something I've kept from them. That'll be hard enough without a witness."

"I can wait outside."

"No, please. Let me handle this. No arguments."

She could see he didn't like it, but he didn't debate the issue.

"What about after?" he asked.

"I have to get to Voodoo. We're finalizing plans for the winter holiday season. But call me if you have anything, and I'll do the same."

His concerned expression cut through her.

"You're going to do it, aren't you?" he demanded. "You're going to place yourself in jeopardy. You agreed we would do this together, Grace."

"One thing at a time, please. I do need to go to work. As to anything else...I'll be cautious." She knew how to hide what she didn't want other people to see. If she got a reading off Raphael—or any other suspect—he or she would never know. "Go take care of things at the office. See if you can find out what's going on with the fingerprint report."

Nodding, Declan backed off.

Even so, Grace felt a little guilty as they left the apartment. He flagged a taxi, but she refused a ride.

"I need time. I need to think on my way there."

His jaw clenched and unclenched. "Be careful."

Understanding his concern, she waved him off and centered herself.

Hoping to find opportunities for psychic connections, she got on a bus that would connect with the St. Charles streetcar. Even this early the bus was packed with people. No place to sit. Too many elbows jostling her. Too many voices filling her head. Too many minds to read.

She was soon on overload again and there was no way to step out of the path of the visions that kept coming and coming. It was like hearing multiple voices, each speaking in a different language.

And now she couldn't turn them off.

Thankfully, the streetcar proved to be more sedate since it was heading away from the business district rather than toward it. Grace was able to have a seat and her private thoughts and the chance to compose herself the short ride into the Garden District.

Still, she was finding it harder to focus.

Harder to breathe.

A problem that multiplied when she got off and walked the few blocks to her family home.

Frozen before the imposing structure, Grace stared at the familiar white columns, at the twelve-foot-high doors, at the old swing on the veranda, as if studying the house was going to change what she would experience inside. Telling herself she could do this—that she could take whatever was coming—she practically ran up the few steps and rang the bell.

Mama answered, dressed for work in a dark pantsuit and a brilliant white blouse. When she saw her daughter, she seemed shocked. "Grace, what in the world are you doing here at this time of the morning? I didn't even know you woke up this early."

"Normally I don't, but I need to talk to you."

"I have an early day, darlin'—can't this wait?"

Warmth crept up Grace's neck as she said, "No, Mama, it can't. It's that important."

"All right." Mama stepped back, letting her by. "I was just finishing breakfast. Go in the kitchen."

"Is Corbett there?"

"Your brother is in Baton Rouge."

Great. She would have to do this twice. She headed for the kitchen with its attention to the old and the new. The cabinetry was old mahogany and there was a butler's pantry, as well. But there was also a center island.

"Coffee?"

"Sure."

Grace slid onto a stool at the island and stared at Mama's plate. Just looking at the half-eaten food was enough to make her stomach cramp.

Mama took her seat and slid a mug toward her, saying, "Here you go, darlin'…now what's so all-fired important?"

Grace took a swallow of the chicory coffee for courage. "Mama, I know I'm not like you or Corbett, but I never meant to hurt you."

Mama's forehead pulled in a frown. "I never thought you did, darlin'. Where is this conversation headed?"

"I didn't do anything on purpose, Mama, I swear. And I've tried to fix things, but I think they've gone too far." Grace felt tears well in her eyes. "That's why I have to tell you, so you'll be forewarned."

"You're scaring me, Grace." Mama put down her fork. "Out with it. What in the world has happened?"

"Someone put a hidden camera in the dressing room at the photography studio."

"Oh."

"The other day, I found a print of this suggestive photograph of me at my apartment door." Grace tried to catch her breath as her mother's mouth formed a large O. "I—I'm being blackmailed."

Hesitating only a second, Mama said, "My Lord, I'll get the best detective in the department on the case right away."

Which as a top prosecutor, she certainly could do.

"No! You can't," Grace said. "Don't you see— then it'll get out for sure. Declan is a private investigator. I hired him to help me. I need to handle this, Mama, try to keep this quiet. But just in case…"

"In case?"

"The blackmailer put the photo on a Web page. He didn't launch the site yet. He says if I give him five hundred thousand dollars, he won't."

"You plan on giving him this money?"

"I don't have this money. I don't have my trust fund yet, remember, and while I make a nice income, my bank account isn't that healthy."

"So you want money from me."

"No, that's not why I'm here. Even if I did give over the money, I don't believe he'd keep his word. I kept this from you to protect myself, as well as you and Corbett. But then I realized that you both had a right to know in case it went wrong. If the photos get out, they could affect your political campaigns. Larry Laroche and Helen Emerson are among the suspects."

"What?"

"Declan and I aren't sure, but we can't rule them out. You have to believe me, Mama, when I tell you we've been trying to deal with this so that this situation wouldn't harm your political career. Yours or Corbett's. I can take whatever they can dish out, but I won't let this hurt you. I'm sorry I've been a coward about telling you."

"Just because someone got a shot of you in the nude—"

"Not nude. Worse."

"What can be worse?"

"I'm dressed, Mama. But it looks like…I'm posed so…well, it's not good."

"I see."

"So if you want to disown me, I—I'll understand."

"Disown you?" Mama's voice went shrill. "What I want to do is take the person responsible for scaring you like this and rip out his fingernails, one at a time."

"Really?" Grace felt tears spring to her eyes.

"My poor baby," Mama murmured, putting her arms around Grace. "My poor darlin' girl."

Shocking Grace into seeing more.

Mama wraps an arm around her waist and beams

at her. She waves with her free hand until Declan joins them. Mama embraces him, too.

When Mama let go, the vision faded.

Grace couldn't remember the last time her mother had soothed her about anything. Then again, normally, she wouldn't show any weakness Mama could use against her.

"You're not angry with me?"

"Oh, I certainly *am* angry with you, but not because a photo was taken of you that might interfere with my political ambitions. I'm angry because you didn't think you could come to me. Because you didn't trust me to believe in you and because you don't trust me to do anything about it."

"*I'm* doing something. I'm using my…ability… to figure out who is responsible. And Declan is helping. He has a computer wiz on it."

"And when you figure out who did it and why…what then?"

"I'm not sure yet."

Mama shook her head and sighed. And then she got that steel in her voice that told Grace she wouldn't put up with any arguments. "I'll give you another day, but if you can't pull this off, the ball is in my court. And if you do get something, you will let me know the blackmailer's identity and turn over any evidence, so that I can have him arrested. The photographs can be kept from the media. And if they aren't, your brother and I will deal with the fallout then. You are my daughter, and you are more important to me than any election."

Words Grace never thought she would live to hear.

She couldn't believe how much she'd misjudged her mother. So much so that she'd made sure they hadn't communicated honestly in years. They didn't have to agree on everything to love each other. She knew that. Even so, she'd never considered Mama would be on her side in this instance.

"I'm so, so sorry, Mama."

And she didn't mean about the photos.

NEEDING SOME TIME to build her confidence before showing up at Voodoo, Grace window-shopped her way up Magazine Street.

Her visit with Mama had been more emotional than she'd imagined, and the walk did her good. Plus it gave her the opportunity to practice her gift one person at a time. No longer having to concentrate on her subject's senses as she'd had to do the night before, she found reading strangers much easier than she'd expected.

An antiques dealer who gave Grace her card was thinking about a lucrative sale.

A kid who literally ran into her on the sidewalk was dreading a doctor's appointment.

Given one person at a time, she was able to

harness the psychic energy…assuming that everything she "read" was correct. That was a problem she wasn't sure any amount of practice was going to help. Hopefully her instincts wouldn't lead her wrong again.

Even though she still had that worry, Grace was feeling much better by the time she entered the Orleans Exchange building and headed up to the second floor.

"Miss Grace, there you are," Eula said. "Mr. Raphael is lookin' for you."

Grace paused at the security desk. "Is he upset about something?"

"Don't think so. Just wanted you to know to see him straight away."

Nodding, Grace took a better look at Eula's desk, which held nothing but a telephone and a monitor that flicked between cameras aimed at the building entrance and the loading dock. "You know, I never realized you didn't have a computer before."

Eula laughed. "That Mr. Raphael is too damn cheap to buy anything he don't think we need."

"I guess he figures you have no use for a computer. It surprises me, though." She glanced up to the Voodoo offices.

Eula shrugged. "There's always the one on the loading dock."

"The computer is out in the open?"

"Nah, you know that little office to the side—it's in there."

Actually, Grace hadn't known about the office because she'd never been in the loading dock area, which was behind the restaurant on the ground floor.

She patted the other woman's hand before leaving.

She seems impatient as she looks down a hallway, then turns to a man, back turned, sitting at a computer, working an e-mail program.

Grace blinked as the image vanished as quickly as it had appeared.

Who had that been at the computer? And had he innocently been checking his own e-mail or had something darker been going on?

Flustered, she said, "I'd better find Raphael."

Her mind was on Eula as she entered the designer's offices, however. Declan was fairly certain the messages had come from one of the building owner's computers. She simply needed to confirm the ISP and the IP address on Raphael's computer and on the one on the loading dock. Now that seemed it would be easier accomplished than she'd imagined.

If, indeed, it turned out the IP address belonged to the loading dock computer, then the hard part would be figuring out who had used it for nefarious purposes.

Entering Voodoo, she smiled at the young receptionist. "Morning, Laurie."

"Oh, Grace! Raphael—"

"Wants to see me first thing. I know."

Grace headed straight for the designer's private office and found him with his assistant.

"…throw the water-damaged bolts into the loading dock Dumpster."

"Are you sure you want to do that?" the assistant asked. "That's a lot of fabric to toss. Maybe we can salvage some of it."

"Raphael does not use goods that are not perfect."

"Whatever you say."

The assistant rushed past her, drawing the designer's attention to her presence.

"Ah, Grace, there you are."

"I understand I'm in demand this morning. Is something wrong?"

"No, nothing other than ruined fabric." He waved the tragedy away with an impatient hand. "Magda is reworking another design and Raphael wants to make sure it fits you the way it should. And that it has your approval."

Tension flowed out of Grace. "My approval?" This was the Raphael she appreciated.

"Things have been difficult lately," he said. "Apologies…I want Voodoo to run smoothly."

He wrapped an arm around her shoulder and gave her a squeeze that shifted her focus.

Larry Laroche wraps an arm around Raphael's shoulder and grins at him.

Zapping herself back to the present, Grace started. Why was he thinking of Larry Laroche? And the way Laroche had snaked an arm around Raphael...surely they weren't having a thing. Laroche was married and as far as she knew, playing with Jill Westerfield. Did Raphael and Laroche have some secret relationship? Is that why he'd been so sharp with her the past few days?

"Well, I'd better go find Magda."

"Good. Good."

When she got to the seamstress, Magda was in the middle of working on a particularly intricate part of the gown.

"Oh, that's going to be stunning," Grace breathed. It was another diaphanous creation that would make her look seminude. But contrary to the way she'd felt the day before, she was looking forward to wearing it. "How soon can I try it on?"

"Check back with me in an hour."

"No problem."

Now what? She could go find Max, see what was on the photographer's mind. Or she could go find the loading dock computer and see what was stored on it.

Could she get to the computer and learn its secrets without getting caught?

Grace called Declan. "Do you have the IP address handy? Apparently, there is a computer I didn't know about in the loading dock office."

"But if the computer is in some place that's accessible to anyone—"

"I know. Anyone could get on it. Anyone and any *thing*. Like the photographs. Maybe I can find the damn files and destroy them."

"What about copies?"

"Overload," she warned him.

"All right. One thing at a time."

"Right. Give me the information I need."

Declan read off the number and she wrote it down on a scrap of paper.

"I'll need directions to get to it, as well."

Declan told her how to find the IP address and then said, "Maybe you should wait for me. I can be there in half an hour—"

"I can do this myself." Grace slipped the paper with the directions into her jacket pocket. "The sooner we know something the better."

"You won't take any chances, right?"

"This building is full of people, Declan. What can happen?"

"One of them can catch you. Maybe the wrong person."

"I'm a good actress. Lots of practice. And I'll keep my cell phone handy."

Though he made a sound of exasperation, he said, "All right. Call me if you find anything."

"That goes unsaid."

"Right away. I want to know you're okay. And in the meantime, maybe you should turn your cell on vibrate in case a call comes in so you don't alert the media."

Grace clenched her jaw. Didn't Declan think she could do anything right without his input?

"I already did."

"Be careful, Grace. I don't want anything to happen to you."

Realizing he was serious—and seriously worried—she said, "I don't want anything to happen to me, either."

Ending the call, she went through the reception area.

Laurie looked up from her computer. "Leaving already? That was quick."

"I'm not even started for the day. Magda was busy, so I'll be back shortly. Should anyone ask…"

"Oh, okay."

Laurie was already concentrating on her work.

Grace slipped out of the office silently, so as not to alert Eula, who sat with her back turned. Because a camera was trained on the security dock entrance, Grace had to get to that office from inside the building if she didn't want to chance Eula's seeing her.

Grace's gaze went straight to a door between Voodoo and Gotcha! She'd never checked it out before, but the door was marked with an exit sign overhead. She would bet her next paycheck it led down to the loading dock. Opening it carefully, she froze when the hinges creaked, but apparently the noise wasn't enough to alert the security guard. Still, it was enough to alert her pulse, which was rushing double-speed. As quietly as possible, she slipped through the opening and made sure the door closed behind her.

Listening intently for other signs of life, she made her way down the stairs. The only sounds she heard other than her own unnatural breathing were kitchen noises coming from the ground floor restaurant as staff got ready for the lunch crowd.

Grace got to the bottom of the stairway, paused and took a good look ahead. From the outside entryway next to the loading dock, light shone in along the hallway. Nothing moving there. Swallowing hard, she took another step forward and could see the vertical loading dock doors were down, so there was no activity here, no reason for anyone to be around.

Even so, she moved cautiously until the freight elevator came into view. It stood open, but no one was around. Raphael's assistant had already been and gone. Clouds of loose colorful fabric half filled the Dumpster that had been pulled up against the loading dock platform.

A big breath and a hope that no one would be back to do anything about them bolstered her courage.

She swung around the corner to the small office and peered in through the window to make sure it was empty before opening the door and taking herself in.

The computer sat there mocking her.

Not about to let anything intimidate her, Grace sat, brought up the display and followed Declan's instructions. In barely more than a minute, she was able to verify the IP address that matched the one connected to the e-mails from the blackmailer.

The e-mails had been sent from this computer!

Heat flushed through Grace. She wanted in the worst way to march upstairs and face down Raphael. But what if he wasn't guilty? Any of the tenants could have gotten to this computer. Then again, why would they?

The image she'd had of Eula and the unidentified man at the computer came to her. But surely it couldn't be the security guard—she was always so polite. Grace would swear Eula really liked her. Eula would have to be a great actor to betray her and seem natural with her afterward.

Then, again, what reason would Raphael have to blackmail her?

Unable to make that call, Grace pulled up the system's search engine and spent a few minutes entering variations on her name to see if it would come up with anything. *Nada*.

She fed in the photo extension and a list of lots…dozens…hundreds of photos started popping up on the screen faster than she could keep up. The photos themselves opened.

Grace watched the screen scroll downward.

There they were. One after another after another. Dozens of photos of her taken wearing the bad-vibe bustier while fantasizing about Declan. Even more of her dressing and undressing.

Fetching her cell phone, she speed-dialed Declan. "What did you find?"

"It's the right IP. And I'm looking at the files of my photos. What do I do now?"

"Get out of there."

"Not until I can get proof." What she wanted was to delete them, but she knew that wouldn't be her wisest move—if they were missing, it would simply alert the blackmailer. She wouldn't doubt he had others, perhaps stored on the camera's memory media. She searched the desk, then swore. "I can't find a damn disk!"

Declan told her what to do instead, ending it with, "Hurry and get out before you get caught."

"I'm already hurrying. I need to get back upstairs anyway—they'll be looking for me."

Disconnecting, she got down to business, her mind whirling. And as the computer worked, she searched the drawers of the desk until she found what she was looking for—a set of building keys.

Mama had said she needed evidence. Having copies of the photographs was only part of it. It proved someone was taking naughty pictures of her, but not who, and not why.

Tonight, no matter what she had to do, that's exactly what she was going to find out.

Chapter Fifteen

Declan was ready to tear out of his office in search of Grace when she finally waltzed through the front door. For once, the energy radiating from her was positive.

"Finally!" he said. "I thought I was going to have to send out search dogs." It took all his restraint not to pull her into his arms and kiss her in relief.

"You know I had to finish up a fitting at Voodoo. I told the receptionist I'd be back and I didn't want Raphael getting suspicious. I assume you got everything I sent?"

Declan nodded and moved to his inner office. "All neatly stored in cyberspace on my account."

"I got something else from the loading dock office." Gazing at him intently, she reached into her pocket and pulled out a key ring and jingled it.

"The keys to the kingdom?" Already he didn't like it.

"One of these matches the loading dock office

door lock, another the freight elevator lock. I would have tried the loading dock entrance, but I would have been on candid camera, and I've had enough of that action."

Not having to work too hard to know what she was up to, Declan unclenched his suddenly tense jaw. "How long can you get for illegal entry?"

"How long can someone get for blackmail?" she countered. "I'll bet the keys to the Voodoo offices and even to Raphael's apartment are here."

Throwing himself in his desk chair, he chose not to argue with her. Perhaps using the keys would never be necessary. "I got some information that's pretty illuminating."

"As in?"

"A connection between Raphael Duhon and Larry Laroche," he said. "They're second cousins once removed."

Grace started. "I've never heard Raphael mention him."

"Could be because he knows it would upset you."

"I saw them together in a vision—Raphael and Laroche. I thought maybe they were having a thing. Even though they're distant cousins, apparently they're close in real life."

"Added to the questionable photos we found in Raphael's profile…"

Grace shook her head. "I just don't see a man like

Raphael hanging outside my apartment. Or chasing me into a parking lot to frighten me."

Declan had been having the same problem. The surge of positive energy he'd felt from Grace had already dissipated to be replaced by a whopping dose of anxiety. That Raphael might be the guilty one, after all, tore her up inside.

"Everything is pointing to Raphael," Declan said just as the computer dinged, alerting him to a new e-mail coming in. "Hold on. Ian said the report on the fingerprints would come through for sure today."

Grace rushed to his side to watch as he opened the e-mail.

"Yep, this is it." He quickly scanned the contents. "Those fingerprints on the notes to you were left by Bergeron Prejean."

"Bergeron? The only man I know by that name is the janitor at our building."

Declan clicked on the link and the browser opened to a page that showed a copy of the fingerprints and his photo—definitely the same man they'd seen when they'd gone to Gotcha! to find the hidden camera. The report included a rundown of Bergeron's criminal history.

"He was just released from prison…" Declan said as he scanned the information. "He was sentenced to four years for armed robbery…eighteen months time served."

"So he gets out of prison, finds a job as a janitor and then decides to blackmail me."

"If he really *is* a janitor," Declan said, searching his desk for the list of building workers. "I didn't see his name on that list you gave me."

Grace leaned into him to see the paper he lifted from the desk. "You're right. No Bergeron…"

"I overheard Raphael warning Eula not to let her brother back in the building. He accused her of giving the man free rein around the place." Finding what he was searching for, he said, "Here it is." Declan tapped an entry on the list. "Eula's last name is Prejean."

"So he's her brother." Grace fell into the chair next to his desk as if the stuffing had been knocked out of her. "When I touched Eula earlier, I saw her looking at a man's back—he was at a computer."

"Did you see the man's face?"

"No, nothing. I barely got a glimpse of the vision and then it was gone."

"Let me check something out." Instincts humming, Declan ran a search on Bergeron Prejean. Lots of links came up. Scanning them quickly, he clicked on one. "Here it is."

"What?"

As the article about Bergeron's trial came up, Grace rose and moved next to him. Trying to ignore the way her closeness affected him, Declan skimmed the text.

"There it is. Motive. Your mother is the one who prosecuted him."

"Oh, Lord…we have him. Now all we need is to prove it. Mama said if we could get proof, she could take care of everything."

"What if it's not Bergeron?"

Though the proof seemed to be right in front of him, as a former cop, Declan knew that what might constitute proof could be misleading. He glanced over the rest of the report on Bergeron. He'd committed a few petty crimes, nothing more revealing. Of course that didn't mean he hadn't committed other crimes for which he hadn't been caught. Still, his instincts told him there was more to it than was obvious.

"I mean, Bergeron could have sent the notes," he explained, "but someone else could be blackmailing you. Two different things. Raphael has just as much motive, if not more."

"Then I'll find the truth."

"I might think they were in it together if Raphael hadn't told Eula her brother wasn't welcome in the building. Or maybe that was simply for effect. He didn't want to be seen with a criminal he was aiding."

They talked about it over a quick lunch of crawfish Etouffée that had been delivered just before she'd arrived. As Grace told him what she wanted to do, Declan thought he'd never seen her so animated, so passionate. She knew exactly how she wanted to play this out. Whatever fear she'd had seemed to have been wiped out by her sense of outrage and determination.

He didn't love Grace's plan, but it might work. If they nailed the villain before he launched the site, they could stop the damage. And Declan would be her backup. He would see that nothing happened to her.

Still…

"I'm the one who should go into the building," he insisted. "I *am* the private investigator."

Grace shook her head. "I didn't start this, but I am going to finish it. Besides, if I get caught in the building, I have a reason to be there. You don't. And I need you as backup—my secret weapon."

Her logic was stellar. The warning in his gut not so much. "I don't want anything bad to happen to you."

"You keep saying that…like it would be your fault."

Declan stared at Grace for a moment. Could he tell her about the family curse? Would she believe him? They didn't exactly have a conventional relationship. Or a personal relationship for that matter. Things had gone so fast.

No doubt she was attracted to him, but did she hope for more?

Whether or not Grace wanted to be with him, against everything he believed in, every vow he'd made, Declan wanted her in every way. He couldn't think of anything—or anyone—else. As she would be the object of Sheelin's revenge, Grace deserved to know in case he'd already poked the prophecy.

"If something bad happens to you, it would be my fault."

Grace shook her head. "Just because you're the professional doesn't mean—"

"No, not that." As much as he didn't want to tell her, he had to warn her. "Because I'm cursed."

Grace reached across the counter to take his hand. On contact, she started and locked gazes with him.

He could feel her reading him!

Not wanting to put anything specific in her head—he figured sometimes people made what they believed would happen come true—Declan went still and tried to clear his mind, not that it would do any good. She would see what she would see. What was in his mind might not be relevant.

Grace's breath caught in her throat. Her confusion and uncertainty washed over him.

"Declan, you need to explain."

She didn't need to clarify. The shift in her was so obvious that he knew she'd seen something that scared her. Reluctant as he was to tell her, Declan didn't feel he had a choice any longer.

"It started a long time ago, Grace, nearly a century," he began. "With Donal McKenna and a woman named Sheelin O'Keefe. They had an affair, but Donal didn't return Sheelin's deep affections. He fell in love with another woman and married her, after which Sheelin, who claimed to be both faerie and witch, damned his children and his children's children. Her prophecy holds nothing good for the McKennas in our family."

"Surely you don't believe in curses."

"An odd thing for you to say, Grace, considering the power of your touch." Declan then decided to tell her something he rarely talked about. "My own mother died such a death. A mysterious fall when she was pregnant with me. She was already dead when the doctors took me from her womb. Da always held that against me. Or perhaps I should say between us."

Declan could sense Grace's shock and something else. Something that made him uneasy.

"I'm afraid I don't understand what this has to do with me," she said.

"My heritage is to find sorrow in love, Grace. Should I act on my feelings, I would put my loved one in mortal danger."

"Is that why you left New Mexico?"

Had she touched him, he would have thought she'd had a vision. "Her name was Lila Soto. When I realized I had deep feelings for her, I knew I had to protect her."

"So you love her."

"No. I mean, now I realize that I cared for her, had feelings for her, but no, she wasn't the love of my life."

Grace opened and closed her mouth, then opened it again. "A-are you saying you love *me?*"

"I'm saying I *can't* love you. *Won't* love you. I won't destroy you." The words left a bitter taste of untruth in his mouth. He might be able to control what he wanted the world to believe, but he knew what he felt. The untruth of it filled him with guilt. "If I had known what would happen, I would never have let things go as far as they did the other night. But we didn't even know each other at the time."

"No, we didn't." She rose and backed off in a cloud of bewilderment and disappointment. "We still don't—or I guess I don't know *you*—so put your worries away, Declan McKenna. You're not responsible for anything that happens to me tonight."

He reached for her but she avoided his hand. "Grace—"

"I'll call you later to confirm our plans. Have my bill ready. When this is over, I want to make sure we can make a clean break."

With that, she headed for the door.

"Grace, wait!"

She was already gone.

Declan was hard-pressed not to go after her. A clean break. Like he'd done with Lila. Yes, that would be best, though the thought left him feeling bereft. Not yet, though. Not until this was finished and he knew that Grace was safe.

Grace would cool down and then they would talk things through—he simply had to give her some time.

SICK INSIDE, Grace decided not to return to Voodoo. Raphael undoubtedly wouldn't guess what she had learned—she'd been able to smile in the face of adversity since she was a child—but she didn't want to test herself right now. Not when her trust was so compromised.

Stopping at a nearby café, she ordered chicory coffee, then called Raphael to excuse herself.

"I'm afraid I have a family crisis to take care of, so I won't be there this afternoon."

"This is not a good time…" He paused, and she thought he would object until he said, "but of course I understand."

"If I can get away earlier than I expect," she said, purposely sounding reluctant, "I could come in later, perhaps sometime this evening."

"No! I have plans for the evening and will be tied up until very late."

Until midnight? Something was bothering him. Good that he'd be gone. She could get into his apartment, then, and search it for evidence.

"Tomorrow, then," she said.

About to flip her phone closed, Grace noticed

she'd had a call from her brother a short while ago. It must have come through when she was someplace without reception. He'd left a voice mail.

"Grace, I just got back from Baton Rouge. Mama filled me in on what's happened to you. Some pervert is blackmailing you. Call me! I'll be home for the rest of the day."

At least she wouldn't have to tell her brother herself, Grace thought, flipping her cell closed. She didn't want to discuss this on the phone, certainly not in a public place.

The waitress brought her coffee and Grace thanked her and paid. But all the while her mind was elsewhere.

Trust had always been an issue with her, ever since the Terrence/bra incident. She hadn't trusted a man enough to chance her heart. She hadn't even trusted her own family to support her. Corbett had trusted Naomi and look what she had done to him. And now Declan to her.

How could Declan have kept everything he'd just told her to himself, especially after hiding the fact that he was psychic? Why couldn't he have told her everything at once rather than hiding what most affected him?

A family curse…a mother who'd died under mysterious circumstances…a woman he'd loved…

He'd had the opportunity to tell her everything before, but he'd held back. And now he couldn't, *wouldn't* love her because of some ridiculous prophecy?

Or was it really because of this Lila Soto?

Grace had known Declan's reason for leaving his home and family in New Mexico must have something to do with a woman. Obviously he still loved this Lila. If he'd only told her about the other woman before, she could have kept her feelings in check, saved herself grief.

Who was she kidding? Declan had unlocked her—she'd had no choice in that or in anything else that had happened between them.

Still, she should have known that Declan McKenna wasn't for her…

Only part of her had thought he was. That he was different. She'd stupidly fallen head over heals with a man who tested her trust. In a weird way, it was the bra incident all over again.

She hadn't thought her heart could be broken twice.

Finishing her coffee quickly, Grace headed for her brother's place. Maybe talking to someone who'd gone through the same thing would make her feel better.

Corbett lived nearby in an old warehouse building that had been converted into loft-style condos. The ten-minute walk gave her enough time to calm down before she got to his apartment door.

"Grace," he said, pulling her inside and giving her

a brotherly hug. "You've got to be going through hell. I know Mama is. She's fretting that you won't let her take over."

Grace pulled out of his arms and moved into his living room, perfectly neat, perfectly put together in browns and tans by a designer. Perfectly boring to her. How could he stand having a sister who was his complete opposite?

"I'm hoping this will end tonight," she said, sitting on the sectional.

"That's when the blackmailer demanded the money?"

She nodded. "At midnight."

He took a seat next to her. "Start from the beginning."

So she had to tell him everything anyway, starting with the notes and ending with all she and Declan discovered about their two remaining suspects, Raphael and Bergeron.

Corbett listened intently through her whole story, then asked, "So what does this Declan McKenna mean to you?"

Her throat tightened. She didn't want her brother to know about her disappointing personal life. "He's been a friend."

"He looked like more than a friend at the fundraiser."

"That was the idea. He was supposed to."

"You might fool other people, Grace—maybe even Mama—but you don't fool me."

"Whatever I might feel doesn't matter. He can't— no, *won't*—love me."

Corbett laughed. "I doubt he has that choice. It doesn't matter what our brains tell us, Grace—our hearts have a mind of their own. That's been my personal hell for the last five years."

Just then, she noticed something on the coffee table—an old snapshot of Corbett with Naomi. One side of his face was pressed into her long, dark hair as if he were trying to inhale her very essence. Her smile was odd—uninvolved—as if she had something to celebrate, but not with the man who held her.

Why had Corbett pulled out the photograph of the woman who'd betrayed him? His personal hell—did that mean he went over and over and over it? Would she?

"Is that why you haven't found another woman to care about?" Grace asked, picking up the photo. "Because Naomi still has your heart?"

"She did for a long time. I was just saying goodbye." He took the photo from her, ripped it in two and dropped it into a trash basket. "I'm finally done with her."

"Because of Jill Westerfield?"

Corbett grinned. "She *is* an interesting woman."

"She's also a reporter."

That sobered him. "What?"

"You didn't know?"

"She told me she was just starting her own public relations business, the reason she was at the fund-raiser with Laroche. Maybe she's picking up work wherever she can until her business is in the black."

"So you *have* been seeing her." Grace hoped her brother would be smarter this time.

"We had drinks. Once."

Worried because her brother got garrulous under the influence, she asked, "What did you talk about?"

"She's not Naomi, Grace."

"She's doing a feature on Voodoo for the *Rising Sun*. She interviewed me yesterday and she didn't just stick to questions about the business."

"She asked about me?"

"There's just something about this woman…I don't like her."

"You didn't like Naomi, either."

His tone made Grace start. "I was right about Naomi, though. You blame me for what happened?"

Corbett sighed. "No, of course not. And nothing happened between Jill and me, Grace, so just relax. I asked her out and she said she was too busy working."

Grace leaned her head on her brother's shoulder. "We make a real pair when it comes to romance."

Not that she was having any after today.

A thought that saddened her deeply.

IT WAS AFTER DARK when Ian arrived at Vieux Carré Investigations. He started when he saw Declan at the front desk.

"You didn't leave yet?"

"I need some equipment," Declan said. In truth, he had nowhere to go, not until it was time to pull off Grace's plan.

"You've been waiting for me?" Ian asked. "Why didn't you just call?"

"I'm waiting for Grace to call."

He suspected he'd be waiting a long time if she wasn't planning on breaking into Raphael's apartment this evening. Thinking someone else ought to know what was going on in case something went wrong, he told Ian about Grace's plan for the evening.

"Hell, man, you're letting her take the lead? Are you crazy?"

"I don't have much choice. If I try to stop her, she'll just fire me and go on her own."

Ian perched a hip on a desk. "How about exerting some *personal* influence?"

"What influence? I told her I couldn't love her."

"So you told her about the prophecy. What did she say?"

"She had the idea I betrayed her somehow by not

telling her before. Or maybe it was because I told her about Lila. She walked out on me."

"And you didn't go after her?"

"For her own good."

"Let's get you that equipment," Ian said.

Ian led the way to his office where he pulled keys from his pocket to open the supply closet door. That's where he kept his electronic toys.

"I want to make sure I have constant communication and I want to see where she is at all times."

"No problem."

Ian pulled several items off the shelf, including a Bluetooth communications system that included a tiny camera—Grace could wear it in her ear. Anyone who saw it would think it was part of her cell phone system, but the wireless technology would allow them voice and visual contact. Rather Declan would be able to see what she could see and they could hear each other.

"Once you get her through this situation," Ian said, "what then?"

"What do you expect? I break all ties with her."

"Why, Declan?" Ian frowned. "The dangerous situation will be ended, then, and you'll have nothing further to worry your head over."

Tempting… Ian didn't believe in the prophecy, Declan reminded himself. "What if there's another danger?"

"What if you have some faith and take a chance? Believe in your own power and Grace's to keep danger at bay. Wouldn't it be worth it?"

Declan didn't know what to think. He'd lived his whole life with his mother's death and his father's consequent rejection of him. That had tainted the way he saw life for himself in the future.

He couldn't sort it all out now, though, not when he needed all his focus to keep Grace safe.

Alive.

Otherwise there would be nothing to think about at all.

Chapter Sixteen

With her plan in place, all Grace had to do was wait for the right time. The e-mail would come in at midnight. Using the keys she'd found in the loading dock office to get in the building, she would try to find the blackmailer at work as Declan stayed on the computer pretending to be her, receiving and answering e-mails. But prior to that, she would try to get into Raphael's apartment so she could look for evidence before he returned. She checked the clock. Quarter to ten and no Declan. Her nerves were vibrating by the time the knock finally came twenty minutes later.

Grace swung open the door and steeled herself at seeing him. "I'm ready to go."

"Not exactly." He waved a small case at her. "A little electronics so we can stay connected."

Despite her resolve, Grace couldn't ignore the way her pulse picked up or the way her throat threatened to close on her. She couldn't force her feelings away. Couldn't stop the longing as Declan opened the case and pulled out what looked like a Bluetooth earbud headset.

"The camera is right here, at the tip. I'll be able to see everything you see." Then he drew out a cell phone. "You can turn this on, okay the Bluetooth connection, then put it in your pocket."

"Looks simple enough."

"Let's try it." Declan set down the cell and moved toward her, earbud raised as if he were going to put it on her.

Pulse thundering, Grace ducked away from his hand. "I can do it myself." She snatched the earbud out of his hand without touching him.

After putting it in place, she okayed the Bluetooth on the cell. Seconds later, a picture of her hand and cell appeared on the cell phone's screen. Looking up, she aimed the camera higher and lifted the cell so she could see Declan's face on the screen.

"If you press the button on the left, you can record everything you see," he told her.

She tried it and saw a tiny red light that assured her she was recording. Stopping the recorder, she slipped the cell phone into her pocket.

"Now I'm ready."

Declan's gaze laved warmth through her. This wasn't the look of a man doing business. No matter what he said, he cared about her, Grace realized.

Not that it changed anything between them. Trust was everything to her. Besides, Lila Soto stood between them.

Grace didn't want a man who couldn't give her his whole heart.

Unlocking her gaze from his, she opened the door and waited for him to leave the apartment first so she could lock up.

The drive was silent and uncomfortable, her thoughts filled with Declan and all that they'd shared in the past few days. She didn't understand all those visions she'd had of the future with them happy together—impossible considering the circumstances.

Just like what had happened with Terrence, she thought glumly. She still couldn't trust her psychic gift.

Less than ten minutes later, they were on the street in back of the Orleans Exchange building. A thrill that felt like fluttering butterflies attacked Grace's stomach. The thought of breaking into Raphael's place to look for evidence wasn't a comfortable one, but if there was proof implicating him, she had to find it before Mama took over. She had to make sure that, if he was the blackmailer, he didn't ruin her mother's and brother's political careers.

Declan pulled up his laptop and she keyed him

into her e-mail. Then he connected to her camera. She saw the low-light, hazy picture of the car's dash and the laptop itself on the monitor. He was able to go back and forth between e-mail and camera.

"I'll be watching your every move," he said. "Do whatever you have to so I can get in the loading dock door, if necessary."

"You're not going to come in after me."

"Only if you're in trouble. Or if the communication breaks down."

"Declan—"

"Don't argue with me, Grace. I agreed to do this your way, but only as long as you're safe." His tone brooked no argument. But as she opened the passenger door and slipped out of the SUV, he quickly added, "Whatever happens, I want you to know I do care about you."

Grace's heart thundered. She didn't respond, but her mind roiled. Though Declan cared about her, he didn't—*wouldn't*—love her. No, thinking about it would cripple her emotionally when she needed all her wits together. This wasn't the time to think about anything personal.

Slamming the door, she quickly crossed the loading dock area, at the same time pulling out the keys to the building. They felt inordinately heavy. Nerves. She had to calm down. The first key she tried was a bust. Hands trembling just a bit, she sorted the others and tried to insert the next one in the lock. Nope. The third key hit pay dirt.

The back entrance door swung open and she whispered, "Okay, I pushed the pin so the door won't lock again."

"Good. Don't say anything unnecessary to me. I can see what you see."

The light inside the building was minimal, yet enough to let her make her way to the lobby, then up the stairs. Treading cautiously, she focused on her surroundings, but heard nothing except the rush of her own blood inside her head. There was no night security guard at the desk, of course, but it was possible there was a night guard somewhere in the building.

A stop just before she reached the second floor assured Grace that she was alone. She rounded the banister and circled the stairs that led to the third floor and the Voodoo offices and Raphael's apartment. Taking a shaky breath, she straightened her spine and hurried up the stairs.

When she got to the landing, she first looked through the windows of the office. All dark as expected. About to start trying keys on his apartment door, she heard noise—voices—and realized someone was inside.

"He's home," she whispered to Declan. "Damn! He said he would be busy until very late."

"Maybe he's entertaining."

"Or maybe he's firing up his computer. I should see for myself."

"Grace, don't!"

Not liking his tone, she said, "I'm not turning back until I find out what's going on up here."

"All right," Declan conceded, though he still sounded unhappy. *"What excuse are you going to use for interrupting him this late?"*

"An apology. Raphael wanted me to come back earlier and I told him I had a family emergency."

"Make it convincing."

"My specialty," she said.

Hoping Raphael wasn't having a romantic tryst, Grace rang his bell. Her mouth was dry, her breathing shallow. Her limbs felt like they were made of rubber.

The door opened, and to Grace's shock, she came face-to-face with Jill Westerfield. And the woman was wearing a Voodoo design, one that hadn't been released yet.

Heart thundering, Grace barely held back a gasp. "I'm here to see Raphael." She pushed her way past the reporter into the apartment foyer. Classical music drifted from another room—music to blackmail by?

"Raphael is otherwise occupied, Ms. Broussard."

"What the hell?" Declan muttered via Bluetooth.

Grace tried to ignore the voice in her earbud. "Where is he, Ms. Westerfield?"

"In the dining room." Jill quickly flashed her gaze to the left before zeroing back in on Grace. "But he isn't to be disturbed."

"I'll just bet he isn't," Grace muttered, storming off toward the dining room.

"Wait!" the other woman demanded. "You can't go in there!"

Grace didn't so much as slow down, so it wasn't until she was almost to the doorway that she became aware of the buzz of voices mingling with the music. Was there a whole team involved in the blackmail scheme?

Stopping in the doorway, she realized Jill was directly behind her. But it was the scene in front of her that wrenched her gut.

Rather than being gathered around a computer, a half-dozen men and three women were sitting around a dinner table, their discarded coffee cups and half-filled glasses of brandy indicating they'd just finished dinner. And Raphael sat at the table's head and was so engaged in conversation that he didn't notice her intrusion.

Larry Laroche sat at the other end.

Grace stepped back, almost banging into Jill. Confused, Grace whipped around to face the other woman.

"We had a dinner for Larry's wealthiest supporters," Jill said. "I told you Raphael was busy."

"I see that now." Humiliated, Grace started to back off. "It can wait. I'll talk to him tomorrow. Go back to your guests."

"I'll see you to the door first." Jill took her by the arm and pushed her toward the door.

"It went well," Laroche says, and pulls Jill up against him. "We're good for each other."

Jill rubs up against him. "You're right." And thinks that she's going to get everything she wants.

Reminded of the way Naomi had used Corbett, Grace pulled her arm free. "I can find my own way out."

Praying the other woman wouldn't follow her or make any kind of fuss, Grace headed for the front door, embarrassed by the mistake she'd made, relieved that Raphael wasn't the blackmailer, but disgusted by his support of Laroche, even if the man was related to him.

Worse, Raphael hadn't told her he was supporting the man competing for her brother's seat on the city council.

She waited until the apartment door swung closed behind her and was on the stairs on her way down before talking just loud enough for Declan to hear.

"The blackmailer isn't Raphael." At least she was grateful for something. "That leaves Bergeron Prejean."

DECLAN COULDN'T HELP but get antsy waiting for Grace to get out of the building and rejoin him. He checked his watch. A few minutes until midnight…

A ding alerted him to the arrival of an e-mail.

"Is that it?" came Grace's voice via the computer speakers.

Apparently, she'd heard. "Three minutes early." Declan brought up the missive.

DO YOU HAVE THE MONEY?

"Well, the bastard couldn't be more direct, could he? He wants to know if you have the money." His fingers flew over the keyboard, bringing up information. "Just give me a few seconds to check out the IP and make sure he's really in the building," Declan said, as the full header of the e-mail opened up on the monitor.

"Well?"

"He spoofed the address again. I can't tell for sure."

"Quick, answer him," Grace said. "Make sure you make it sound like it was from me. Keep him busy while I check it out from inside."

"Grace, do you really think this is a good idea? I'm worried that Bergeron might be armed."

A fact that made his stomach lurch even as Grace protested, "I won't face him down. As soon as I see him, I'll let you know. Just type and don't let him off the hook!"

"All right, all right," he muttered, typing as fast as his fingers would let him.

I'm in the process of getting the money, but I need more time. Another twenty-four hours.

Declan fidgeted as he waited for a response. One minute. Two. Three. Too long. There should be a reply by now. His gut was telling him something was wrong. And why hadn't he heard anything from Grace?

What if she'd stumbled on the blackmailer and was in trouble? He switched over to the camera feed. She was in some kind of a corridor.

"Are you all right?"

No answer. And the camera view suddenly became static. What the hell?

About to get out of the car and go after Grace— her safety was more important than any promise he'd made her—Declan stopped with his hand on the car door when a second message from the black- mailer arrived in her in-box. He quickly opened it.

SEVENTY-TWO HOURS MEANS SEVENTY-TWO HOURS. THE PRICE JUST WENT UP. HAVE $750,000 BY MIDNIGHT TOMORROW OR I'LL SEE THAT YOU BECOME THE FAVORITE WEB WHORE OF NEW ORLEANS.

A black rage clouded Declan's vision for a moment, and he couldn't think of a good enough punishment for the person who wanted to ruin Grace's life. He typed a furiously fast reply.

Wait. Let's negotiate. I can barely lay my hands on half a mil.

Apparently Grace hadn't caught up to him yet.

THE LOADING DOCK COMPUTER…that had to be the place where the blackmailer was working. Hearing voices, Grace had pulled into a janitor's closet where she'd frozen.

"Grace, he's offline! Say something if you're all right!"

Fearing she could be heard, she nodded her head instead, giving him a visual clue that he would see on his monitor.

"Okay. Thank God. Are you down in the loading dock area?"

She nodded again.

"I'm going to wait a minute to see if another message comes through. If not, I'm coming after you."

She listened intently and picked up the murmur of conversation. Coming carefully out of the janitor's closet, she slid her back along the wall and concentrated on the voices, one familiar.

"Let's get outta here," Eula said

"Ain't done yet. Hold on to your pants. The bitch has gotta know who's boss. Got one more message to send."

"Hurry."

Anger filled Grace as she moved out into the open so she could see through the office doorway. Eula Prejean's eyes opened wide as the security guard caught sight of her.

Just like in her vision, Eula was standing guard, watching for intruders, while a man with his back to the door sent out an e-mail message.

To her!

"M-Miss Grace…"

"What about the bitch?"

"I'm looking at her, Bergeron."

"What, you print off one of them photos?"

"I mean in the flesh."

The man whirled around and Grace immediately caught a definite resemblance between the siblings. Bergeron's expression was downright mean, however, while Eula simply appeared to be afraid.

"Grace! What the hell are you doing?" Declan asked.

Grace ignored him. "How could you do this, Eula? I thought we were friends."

"We are, Miss Grace. You've always been kind to me—"

"Stop blathering. My sister here is weak. She has a soft spot for you." Bergeron pushed his way out of the office toward Grace. "But don't make that mistake with me."

So Eula had let her brother bully her into helping with the blackmail scheme.

"Grace, get out of there now!"

"Not yet. I have to know the truth." Though Grace's nerves were stretched tight as she backed up, she gave Bergeron her best glare. "Why?" She wasn't going anywhere until he told her.

"Your mama, the saintly prosecutor. Does she know what kind of pictures you pose for?"

"You did all this because she put you where you belonged?"

"She put me behind bars for no reason—I was innocent. I never did no armed robbery. Just got out on parole and I figure your family owes me. Pocket change money to you folks anyhow."

"I told you I didn't have that kind of money."

"You got family money. And now I want more. You're late with the payment and, knowing who

I am and all, I have to go on the run. Now I want a million."

"You're not getting a cent from me!" Grace said. "As a matter of fact, you should go on the run now, while you can, before the police get here."

"If you don't have it tomorrow night, that Web site will be in the news!"

Bergeron Prejean barked a laugh and with uncommon speed, he lunged forward and gave her a hard shove.

"Bergeron, what you doing?" Eula yelled. "You weren't supposed to hurt nobody."

"Grace!" Declan's shout through the earbud nearly deafened her.

Now wanting to escape, Grace got to the door, but Bergeron came after her. No sooner was she on the outside dock than he shoved her again. Harder. Grace stumbled and her rear foot met air. She tried to catch herself, but she couldn't get her balance. A quick look over her shoulder brought the Dumpster coming up fast to greet Grace.

"Shut up, Eula. Just making sure she can't cause me no trouble whilst I clean out those files so I don't leave no evidence."

Grace's landing was softened by that material Raphael had told his assistant to discard. She tried to fight it to find a way out, but the Dumpster's silky contents made her slip and slide all over the place.

It was like walking in quicksand. She kept sinking and couldn't keep her balance.

"Eula, please help me," she begged. "Don't leave me in here."

Down she went again, this time, yards and yards of the fabric threatening to engulf her in a cocoon…to drown her in a sea of silk and satin.

RUNNING TOWARD the back entrance, Declan heard Eula say, "Sorry, M-Miss Grace. Bergeron is my b-brother. I gotta do it his way."

"But he's made a criminal of you," Grace said as she unsuccessfully tried to pull herself out of the Dumpster.

"Like your mama made a criminal of him."

"I'm sick of listening to the bitch squawk!"

Declan turned the corner and Bergeron immediately spotted him. The man's eyes went wide and he broadcast fear all the way to Declan.

"Move, Eula!"

Bergeron shoved his sister out of the way, picked up a length of material and wrapped it around Grace's neck, giving it a jerk so it tightened. As Declan ran up the loading dock steps, Grace made a horrible noise and put her hands to the material as if trying to free herself so she could breathe. Bergeron struck out with a booted foot and kicked

Grace in the shoulder so that she went flying backward and bounced off the side of the Dumpster.

"Bergeron, no!" Eula screamed.

Seeing red, Declan raced toward the man with a war cry. Bergeron was half-turned when he made contact, Declan's shoulder to the blackmailer's solar plexus. Both men went flying into the Dumpster alongside Grace, then were nearly buried in a pile of cloth. Having landed on top of the bastard who'd tried to hurt the woman he loved, Declan shoved his fist into the man's face. Several times.

Even so, Bergeron rose, one hand flashing around Declan's throat, while the other fisted and came flying toward him. An explosion in his head knocked Declan silly just long enough for Bergeron to clamber over him and out of the Dumpster.

Next to him, Grace was making strangled sounds and clawing at the material on her neck. No contest about what he would do first. Declan threw himself next to her and quickly worked out the knot. He didn't take an easy breath until Grace did.

"He's getting away," she croaked. "Go after him!"

"After I get you out of here."

He helped her to her feet and in one smooth motion, hopped out of the Dumpster, bringing her with him.

"You're all right?"

"Go!" She was turning to look at Eula.

Fearing the security guard might have a weapon, Declan hesitated long enough to check.

From somewhere nearby, an engine roared and a vehicle careened down the street. A loud thwack and Eula's screamed "Bergeron!" made Declan turn to see the man's flying body bounce off the edge of the building and hit the pavement even as the vehicle sped away without slowing.

Declan ran to Bergeron, but there was nothing he could do for the man. Bergeron's head tilted crookedly, his ear almost touching his shoulder. No pulse. Eula fell to her knees on the other side of his body and wailed. Declan looked up to find Grace a few feet away—she was on her cell phone.

"Yes, Mama," she was saying as she drew close, "send them in now."

Mere seconds later, the street was crawling with cops. Eula was under arrest and Bergeron was being packed into an ambulance in a zipped black plastic bag.

The blackmailer was dead, and Grace was safe, not just from scandal.

To Declan's everlasting relief, the woman he loved was finally out of mortal danger.

Chapter Seventeen

After the exhausting night she'd spent tracking down a criminal followed by a couple of hours with the authorities that included her mother—not to mention Corbett, who'd come down to provide moral support—Grace thought she might be able to sleep.

Wrong.

She tried and tried, but no matter how hard she wanted to shut down her mind, she could see Declan, the way he'd looked at her before leaving the station. He'd been waiting for her to say something, to stop him.

To tell him that she wanted a real relationship with him when he was the one who'd denied her only hours before?

When push came to shove, Declan had backed her all the way. He'd saved her life—she would have suffocated if he hadn't been there for her. Even so, afterward, she'd said nothing personal, had simply let him go home alone.

A man who'd saved her life deserved her complete trust and he had it. But how could she share him with another woman, even if that woman was merely a memory?

Declan had loved and left Lila for her own good. He'd refused to love Grace for the same reason.

Declan McKenna was honorable and protective and self-sacrificing.

He was also a coward.

If Declan had really loved Lila, he should have stayed in New Mexico and fought for the woman.

The way he'd fought for her the night before, Grace thought.

What was Declan doing now? she wondered, tossing and turning and spinning visions of the way Declan would make love to her if he were here. What good were all those visions she'd had over the past few days? If they didn't come true, what did that say about her gift?

Grace sighed.

She'd used her psychic ability to catch a blackmailer, and now she was done with it.

Wasn't she?

Sunlight sneaked into the bedroom through cracks between the heavy curtains, informing Grace that morning had arrived. Exhausted, giving up the pretense of sleep, she took a shower, then pulled on a pair of loose pants and a T-shirt, comfort clothes that she only wore around the house when there was no one to see her.

Wandering through her apartment, she wondered how she was going to fill her day. It wasn't that she lacked for things to do. She simply had no desire to start something she probably wouldn't want to finish. She certainly didn't want to go to work today.

Voodoo Woman…who was she?

Grace fetched the photo from the bedroom dresser. Was she really this sensual creature or had she been fooling herself like some tourist hiding behind a Mardi Gras mask?

She needed to find out.

Returning to the living area, she knelt on the floor and opened her peacock-and-gold trunk and studied the items that were her past. Picking up the feathered Mardi Gras mask, she set it in front of her face. She could almost feel Grandmama Madelaine's presence, protective arms wrapped around her, lovely southern accented voice spinning tales of the gift they shared. The gift she'd hidden for so long.

"Help me figure it out, Grandmama. Who am I?"

She stared at the two items in pink—shoes and bra. Which one was she? The woman who dared to be different or the one who ran from herself? Trust—something absent in her life for too long. Above all, she owed trust to herself.

Standing, she took the pink bra to the kitchen and dropped it into the garbage can where the memories it invoked belonged. She wouldn't let fear guide her anymore.

Grace Broussard, eccentric and complex—Voodoo Woman—was exactly who she wanted to be. She was going to accept her psychic visions for the gifts they were. And she was going to stake her claim on the man she loved.

Grabbing her keys and wallet, Grace decided to face Declan. She opened the apartment door, and as if conjured, he stood there, scowling at her.

"I've been doing some thinking, Grace. About you and me."

Her already fluttering pulse sped up. "So have I." She stepped back. "Come in."

Declan didn't hesitate. He stopped in the middle of the living room and announced, "You're not in danger anymore."

Closing the door, she said, "Thanks to you."

"Maybe that's how it's supposed to be—the McKenna protecting the one he or she loves from the family curse," Declan said. "Not that it *has* to end in tragedy. I'm sorry I didn't tell you about my past before."

A thrill ran through her. "And I'm sorry I gave you such a hard time. Trust hasn't come easy to me…but I'm going to change all that."

Grace moved into Declan and he slid his arms around her back. He kissed her and kissed her again.

Breathless, she slid out of his arms. "About Lila—"

"Lila is my past."

"But you love her."

"I thought so. I'm not sure anymore. I know I was too wary because of the way my mother died so senselessly. It's possible the first time I thought my heart might be involved, I panicked when I shouldn't have. Of course I cared about Lila or I wouldn't have abandoned my home, my family. But since I met you…you make me feel things she never did. I can't even see Lila clearly in my mind anymore. All I can think about is *you,* Grace. I can't deny it any more. I love *you.*"

"So why are you here, Declan?" Grace's pulse was racing and she was having trouble taking a deep breath. "To give me your farewell?"

He shook his head. "Ian was right. He told me to use my power—and yours. Together. He told me to fight for what I wanted. And I want you." He reached for her and she let him pull her close. "What do you want, Grace?"

Heart thundering, she touched his face, stared into his bedroom eyes. "I want you, too, Declan."

She wanted to be with him, to see the visions come to pass, which wasn't going to happen with them standing in the middle of her living room fully dressed.

She removed her shoes…pants…top…

He followed suit.

Their clothing scattered along the floor, entangled as their limbs would soon be.

He pulled her into an embrace and they sank to the floor together. Thrilled to her toes, Grace lay on her back and slid a hand down her belly to the juncture of her thighs.

"I want you…want to feel you inside me," she whispered. "I want to feel like I'm part of you."

Declan slid his body alongside hers and placed a hand over hers. Nearly ready to come at his first touch, she tugged at him and he moved over her, knees between her thighs. When she felt the pressure at her entrance, she shuddered and opened wider. The sensation of him filling her was nearly more than she could stand. Her hips came up as if of their own volition.

Declan leaned forward and caught her wrists, bringing them up over her head. He tented her with his body, but he didn't move. His bedroom gaze connected with hers and held. Then he began moving slowly, oh so slowly, a gentle rocking, barely noticeable. Pleasure hummed through Grace.

She rolled her hips in an attempt to set the rhythm faster and deeper. He stopped moving.

"You're driving me crazy, Declan McKenna."

"Good."

"Why?"

"Because I want you to want me more than any man you've ever known."

He rolled and brought her with him so she was on top.

Her rocking over him swung her breasts forward so they brushed his face. He drew a nipple into his mouth and suckled her. The sensation from that contact shot to every nerve. Mindless with desire, Grace fought to hold on so they could come together. She stared down into his face as he clung to her breast, working it until her head went light.

His fingers explored below. If he touched her in just the right place, she would surely explode.

She shifted her weight so they rolled together, leaving him on top. Lifting her legs to circle his thighs, she rode his hips. He was panting, now, fighting to hold back.

Smiling, she reached out to touch his face and opened her mind.

He grins down at her...a loopy grin unlike anything she's seen before...he touches her stomach and then covers her face with kisses.

Her heart is so full, she feels as if it's about to burst.

The euphoric feeling lasted beyond the vision, making Grace climb higher than ever before until Declan tensed. Freeing herself with him, she found new meaning in the fireworks in her mind.

SOME HOURS LATER, the phone rang.

Lounging in bed, Declan drowsily watched Grace reach over to get it. Outside, the wind was blowing and the sky darkening with threatening rain. But it was warm and cozy where they were and he couldn't get enough of her. Nor could he resist cupping her breast.

Grace took a look at the caller ID. "It's my brother." She put the receiver to her ear. "Hey, Corbett." As she listened her smile slowly faded. "What?" Then the color in her face faded into a sickly white. "I don't believe it. How?"

Declan rolled out of bed and pulled on his pants. "What's going on?"

"Just a minute, Corbett. Oh, okay. I'll talk to you later, then." She hung up.

Worried as hell, Declan said, "Grace, tell me."

"The Web site. Apparently, Bergeron just launched it."

Thunder cracked and a flare of white light lit the room for a second—portents of more evil in their lives. Rain came down with a rush, battering the apartment house, the drumming sound pushing Declan into action.

Cursing under his breath, he rushed to the living room where he booted up Grace's laptop. With a sheet wrapped modestly around her, Grace followed and sat next to him. He tried to read her, but it was as if shock had left her devoid of emotion. He typed her name into a search engine and immediately found the link. One click and horror became a reality—Grace exposed for the world to see.

"Corbett said he's going to try to get it taken down," she said in a small voice. "Can he do that?"

"Let's think positively."

He pulled her into his arms and felt her shiver.

The only thing Declan was positive about was that, even if Corbett did succeed, thousands would see the damn Web site first. And he feared anything that had once been on the Net was never really gone.

Inhaling Grace's scent, Declan pulled her closer, as if the contact could protect her. He'd thought the woman he loved was out of danger.

But looking at her crumpled expression, he realized there was more than one way to inflict a mortal wound.

"PUBLIC SENTIMENT SEEMS to be with Grace Broussard, our very own Voodoo Woman," the news anchor announced on the midday news.

He hadn't even shown the damn Web site, not even with the special effects to hide the "forbidden" parts. Instead, a photograph of the bitch in a glamorous purple number filled the LCD monitor.

"Her mother, Assistant District Attorney Sandra Broussard, and brother, City Councilmember

Corbett Broussard, are both outraged and vow that whoever is responsible will be held accountable. With a few exceptions, the public stands behind them both."

Then a full glass crashed into the monitor, splashing ice cubes and alcohol everywhere.

"This can't be happening! This was supposed to destroy them, not make them martyrs!"

The plan had been foolproof, carefully planned every step of the way. Attack the most vulnerable member of a moneyed family and get a windfall. And get a little revenge, as well.

Why couldn't the bitch have gone along with the plan?

No, she had to involve that private investigator. She had to ruin everything. Even if Grace Broussard had come up with the money, nothing would have been enough to keep that Web site from going public.

But nothing had gone right the night before.

Nothing but the part where Bergeron Prejean— the only witness—was silenced forever. The authorities called it a hit and run. Exactly as planned.

Now what?

The rest of the plan had backfired.

There was no money.

And rather than shunning Grace and her family, the public was embracing the Broussards as victims!

There was only one thing left to do—make Grace Broussard pay in a very final way.

GRACE HADN'T MEANT to see Eula Prejean again when she and Declan cut through the gray day to the Orleans Parish Criminal District Court to check on Mama. It had stopped raining, and now the fog was rising off the river and snaking along the pavement. Approaching the courthouse had given her pause. The gray building had looked like it was rising out of a smoky Hell.

Exactly what she wished she could do…but was powerless to accomplish.

So there Eula was, sitting on a bench in the wainscoted hallway with her lawyer, a guard standing on the other side. At first, Grace didn't know how to react. Or if she could. She simply felt empty. Useless. Unable to control anything that happened in her life now.

Eula's eyes widened when she saw Grace and she shakily stood and reached out a hand. "Miss Grace, please, can I talk to you a minute?"

Thinking about how Eula had tried to stop Bergeron from hurting her the day before, Grace stopped, but didn't know what to say. Declan's supportive arm around her shoulders tightened. The former security guard looked terrible—her face was swollen from crying. Something in Grace softened—she couldn't help but be sympathetic for Eula's loss. Even if Bergeron had been lower than low, he had been Eula's brother. Grace couldn't even fathom what it would be like to lose Corbett.

"What is it?" she finally asked.

"I-I wanted you to know I'm sorry," Eula said. "I didn't mean for nothin' bad to happen to you."

"You just wanted to expose me and my family with that Web site."

"No! Bergeron didn't commit no armed robbery, and outta prison like that, he couldn't get no job. He just wanted enough money to go somewhere and start over and figured your family owed him. I don't know why he tried to hurt you, Miss Grace, I swear. To escape, I guess. He never did nothin' like that before. He was desperate."

"But he *did* hurt me, Eula. Not only physically. When he launched that Web site, he hurt my whole family."

Even though public sentiment seemed to be on their side, Grace knew her mother wasn't as nonchalant about the situation as she tried to appear.

"Bergeron didn't launch no Web site."

"But he did, Eula. I guess you haven't seen the news today."

"I know what happened, and I'm sorry for that, too." Eula shook her head. "But I'm telling you it wasn't my brother. Bergeron barely knew how to use a computer. He wouldn't know how to do that technical stuff."

"He knew enough to build the Web site," Declan said.

"No, he didn't. He just passed it on, had it on one of them thumb drives. Said someone else put the Web page together."

"Who?" Declan asked.

"He never told me." Eula shook her head and her dark eyes filled with tears. "I'm sorry. I'm sorry."

Grace suddenly had trouble breathing. "Are you saying someone else was involved in the blackmail scheme?"

Eula shrugged. "Honest, Miss Grace, I don't know about no one else. I only know my brother couldn't have made that Web site because he didn't know how."

"WHO COULD HAVE DONE IT?" Grace asked Declan as they walked down the hall to meet her mother. "If not Bergeron Prejean, then who was he working with?"

"One of the usual suspects, I assume." Declan spotted Sandra Broussard speaking to the blond reporter who'd given Grace such a hard time. Grace's mother didn't look all too happy, so the woman must be on her case now. "Trouble ahead."

Even as he said it, Jill Westerfield honed in on them as if she had built-in radar. Grace shrank into him, then, as if collecting herself, pulled away and stood tall.

Wearing a jubilant smile, the reporter said, "Why, Ms. Broussard, I was just going to track you down. A follow-up for the *Rising Sun* feature. Readers will want to know your reaction to the terrible blackmail plot against you."

"No comment, Ms. Westerfield," Grace said in a gracious tone.

A tone that hid irritation, Declan realized. But he was getting stronger vibes from the reporter. She was angry that Grace wasn't cooperating. And there was something else he couldn't quite get.

Jill's eyes glittered behind the horn-rimmed glasses. "I just thought you might want to defend yourself."

"My daughter has nothing to defend, Ms. Westerfield," Sandra Broussard said. "She's the victim here."

The reporter was silent as she assessed the situation, glancing from one woman to the other. Then she said, "Of course she is. My apologies."

Jill Westerfield was anything but sorry. The reporter was pursuing a story, so why did her emotions feel so personal? Declan wondered as she stalked off, brushing against Grace, who looked after the blonde with an odd expression.

Had Grace seen something?

About to ask if she'd had a vision, he held back when Grace gave him a warning flash of her eyes.

Declan knew her mother wasn't aware she was using her ability again any more than she was aware that Grace and he were a couple.

"Thank you for bringing me, Declan," Grace said. "I'm going to have dinner with Mama and Corbett. Call me later, okay?"

"Whatever you need."

Right now she needed time with her mother and brother. Though Declan wished he could stay with her, he understood. Her family didn't even know their relationship had turned personal, so his being there would seem odd.

Besides which, he had some investigating to do back at the office.

As he entered Vieux Carré Investigations ten minutes later, Ian was just leaving for the day. Declan had already filled him in by phone on everything that happened the night before and earlier in the day. He quickly updated him about Eula's claim that Bergeron hadn't had anything to do with the Web site.

"So why are you here instead of with Grace?" Ian asked.

"Continuing the investigation. Have you ever heard of a reporter named Jill Westerfield? She works for the *Rising Sun*."

"Name's not familiar. She new in town?"

"Could be." Probably was if Ian didn't know the name. "I'm going to find out."

"Don't work too late. You need to take care of your woman tonight."

"That's what I'm trying to do, Ian."

A few minutes later, Declan settled down in his office in front of his computer. He ran a search on Jill Westerfield. He'd gotten emotions from the woman far darker than those from Bergeron…more in keeping with the person he'd chased from Grace's building to Bourbon Street. Other than her association with *Rising Sun,* he found nothing about a woman going by the name of Jill Westerfield living in New Orleans.

Huh. How was that possible? Maybe she had just moved to the city. He expanded his search to the whole state…and then to neighboring states where he found multiple references to three women named Jill Westerfield.

By the time he found the article about the reporter from Biloxi, Mississippi, who went missing a couple of months ago on a business trip to New Orleans, the sun had already set and another bout of rain further darkened the skies outside the office windows. Declan glanced back to the computer monitor. A hazy photo of a woman with short, blond hair and horn-rimmed glasses accompanied the article.

Vaguely aware that it was getting late and Grace hadn't called yet, Declan forced himself to stay put until he played out this lead.

Knowing the media always blew up the bad stuff, but didn't always come through with the resolutions to stories if they didn't have any shock value, he decided to call a contact in the police department.

Yes, a Jill Westerfield had disappeared according to Biloxi relatives who'd made a complaint three months ago, but she'd never been found.

Three months…about the same time the reporter started writing for the *Rising Sun*.

Hanging up, Declan sat back staring at the monitor.

Why hadn't the reporter ever let her family know she was all right and living here now?

He enlarged the picture of the blonde, but the photo grew fuzzy. Was this the same woman he'd faced in that courthouse hallway an hour ago or had there been some kind of identity switch? Uncertain, he hit print.

Wanting Grace to take a look, he tried to call her. Her home phone went right to voice mail.

"Hey, this is me calling you. I'll try your cell."

But the cell phone didn't scare her up, either.

Leaving another message that she should call him—telling himself Grace was simply involved with her family—Declan checked his watch. He'd give her a half hour and then try again.

Chapter Eighteen

Dinner had felt forced. Mama and Corbett kept trying to make Grace feel better. They'd even invited Cousin Minny. Grace just wanted to be alone—or better yet, to be with Declan—but she suspected her family's attempt to cheer her in reality kept *them* from depression. No matter that the public seemed to be on their side, Grace knew there would be whispers anywhere they went. People loved to gossip, even about those who'd been victimized.

"We could have coffee or iced tea in the living room," Mama announced, shooing them from the table. "It's Cornelia's day off, so I'll get it myself."

Grace said, "Mama, we can help—"

"Just go sit. All of you. I insist."

Reluctantly, Grace followed her brother and cousin into the living room. Maybe Mama needed a few minutes alone herself. Corbett took the wing-back chair where he'd left his laptop and Minny made herself comfortable on the sofa. Today she was a splash of fuchsia against the flowered upholstery.

Realizing her brother was sneaking a peek at the computer, Grace asked, "Is it still there?" She assumed he would understand she was asking about the offensive Web site.

"Afraid so. It'll probably take a court order to have it removed. If all traces *can* be removed."

"If only we could find out who owns the site."

So far, they'd had no luck. The owner's identity was well hidden. No surprise there.

"Take some comfort that the blackmailer's plot backfired and the public is outraged," Minny said. "For once."

Remembering that Minny had gotten bad vibes from touching the bustier in the first place, Grace asked, "You couldn't by any chance see something about the owner by touching the Web site on the monitor?"

"I'm afraid my powers don't extend to cyberspace. Or electronics in general. I already tried," Minny admitted. "Now if you could line up the suspects in person and I could touch *them*…"

"If we knew who to suspect," Corbett said.

"I still wonder about Larry Laroche." Grace watched her brother carefully and added, "And then, of course, there's Jill Westerfield." Whom she hadn't considered earlier in the crisis because she hadn't had any direct contact with the woman until the interview for the *Rising Sun*.

Corbett's head whipped up, the computer suddenly forgotten. "Grace, I know you don't like Jill—"

"The problem is, *she* doesn't like *me* and makes no bones about it. And I have no idea of why."

"I think you're listening to your imagination."

"No, to Jill herself. She answered the door at Raphael's last night. She touched me…"

"And what did you see?" Minny asked eagerly.

"Jill Westerfield with Larry Laroche—"

"He's her client!" Corbett protested.

Part of her brother still wanted to deny that she and Minny had abilities he couldn't understand. His world was black-and-white, no shades of gray allowed.

"A personal client, then," Grace told him. "She was rubbing up against him *very* personally and thinking that she was going to get everything she ever wanted."

"So?" Corbett wouldn't let it go. "That makes Jill guilty of blackmail?"

"And today," Grace went on, "when she tried to get me to talk in the courthouse, and I wouldn't give her what she wanted, she brushed my shoulder."

"So what did you see, Grace?" Minny asked again.

"Her with Corbett."

Her brother laughed. "Hey, things are looking up."

Grace's stomach tightened. Her brother was turning her reservations into some kind of joke.

"I don't think there's anything positive about it. Her expression…" Grace tried to explain. "You looked happy, Corbett, but she was smiling like she was…I don't know…triumphant."

"Oh, yeah, convict her for smiling at me."

"Don't be too quick to dismiss your sister's instincts," Minny said. "If Grace had a vision, there's a good reason for her seeing what she did. You need to pay attention!"

Grace sighed. "I only wish I saw something more telling."

"I saw something telling on my way over here," Minny said.

"Like what?" Corbett asked.

"I stopped at the Orleans Exchange building, walked around the loading dock…and into the street where Bergeron Prejean was hit by a car."

"And someone was there?"

"No one. But there was dried blood on the pavement."

Grace started. "What did you see?"

"It's what I felt…what Bergeron was thinking as he was hit. He knew the driver."

"Knew…as in the driver hit him on purpose?"

"That's what I would suppose."

"The two of you—listen to yourselves," Corbett muttered. "Making up a case for murder now."

Just then, Mama entered the room carrying a tray with a carafe of hot coffee and a pitcher of iced tea. Grace's cue to back off Corbett. Though Mama didn't show it, Grace knew she was upset as it was. She didn't need to get in the middle between her children.

Realizing Corbett was about to close his laptop, Grace said, "Hey, wait! I haven't checked my e-mail today. What if whoever launched the Web site has been trying to get in touch with me?"

Scowling now, Corbett passed the computer to Grace. On edge, she set it on the table in front of her and opened her e-mail program. Quickly scanning the in-box, she didn't realize she was holding her breath until, finding no additional threat, she let the breath out.

"Nothing from the blackmailer, but there's a message from Declan," she said, wondering why he'd e-mailed her rather than called her.

GRACE—
I TRACKED DOWN A LEAD. THERE'S SOMETHING I WANT TO SHOW YOU. I'M TIED UP FOR A WHILE. MEET ME AT 10 ON THE MOONWALK IN THE AREA BEHIND CAFÉ DU MONDE—THERE'S A BENCH NEAR THE STEPS THAT GO DOWN TO THE RIVER.
DECLAN

Thinking it was an odd request, Grace figured Declan must have a good reason. Maybe whatever he had to show her was there in the open?

Unable to imagine what, she checked her watch. "Declan wants me to meet him at ten, but I still have time for a coffee."

Minny squealed. "Oooh, you're having a tryst…"

"Tryst?" Mama echoed.

Though Grace hadn't intended to talk about her relationship with Declan tonight, Minny had let the cat out of the bag. So over coffee and iced tea, Grace filled in the family with as few details as possible. Mama was not quite as delighted with the match as she'd been when she didn't know Declan was merely a private investigator, but she put up a good front. Corbett said he would wait to pass judgment until he got to know Declan better.

Supportive as always, Minny patted her on the arm and whispered, "I'm so pleased for you, Grace. You've finally come into your own."

"Whatever that means."

"Think of Declan as…well, your new pink shoes."

Chuckling, Grace hugged Minny. Her cousin always knew how to lighten her mood.

Not that the good mood had long to last.

A QUARTER OF AN HOUR LATER, Minny pulled her car over where Front Street ended, as close to Grace's destination as she could get.

"We can park the car and I can come with you," Minny volunteered.

Grace loved her cousin for being so concerned. "I'll be fine. Really." Hopping out of the car, she waved Minny off.

A far more sober Grace refocused herself on the things that had happened to her and on the perpetrator. The rain had stopped, but fog clung to the sidewalks and streets and climbed the lightposts and buildings, making the surroundings surreal. As Grace cut across the train tracks to the Moonwalk, she could hear the storm-swollen river lap heavily toward shore.

Her mind roiled with possibilities.

She tried to imagine Raphael as a murderer, no less a blackmailer, but she simply couldn't believe he meant to harm her. Laroche was a blowhard, base to his political enemies, greedy and not above taking other people's money if he was indeed part of that Ponzi scheme Declan had dug up. He might be a despicable human being, but she didn't see him as the brains behind the operation.

And then there was Jill Westerfield, who seemed to hate her for no reason….

Or was there?

Was the reporter hiding something? Grace wondered.

Reaching the Moonwalk, Grace headed for the

bench near the steps that went down to the water, still some ways ahead. The fog was more prevalent here, making the surroundings look slightly out of focus. The river beat against the shore, sending up a fine spray, probably the reason the area was deserted. Beneath the crash of the waves came the sweet, deep-throated melody of a sax. Likely a street musician over on Decatur. Rather than soothing her, the sound oddly put her on edge.

Her thoughts drifted back to Jill, to the vision she'd had at Raphael's place. Jill's self-satisfied smile so telling that Grace couldn't quite forget it…maybe because it reminded her of something. *Someone.* Focusing inward, she stopped for a moment when it came to her. The snapshot on Corbett's coffee table…the one of him with Naomi…that same self-satisfied smile…

"Oh, no," she choked out.

Surely it couldn't be. And Corbett simply couldn't be so unwitting.

Still trying to sort it out in her mind, Grace suddenly became aware of the sound of steps approaching. Glancing over her shoulder, Grace got a quick glimpse of a dark figure behind her—one that reminded her of the person who'd chased her through the Marigny a few nights before—and then the fog thickened, swallowing the dark phantom.

Pulse rushing, Grace had a bad feeling about this.

She opened her purse and felt for her cell phone so she could call Declan, but the cell wasn't there, and suddenly she could see it on the breakfast bar where she'd put it down while getting ready to leave that morning. No wonder he'd never called—he hadn't been able to get hold of her. She picked up her pace after another nervous glance over her shoulder, but the thickening fog kept her from seeing anyone else.

Even as she sped up, so did the footsteps following her.

A clear spot ahead revealed the bench near the staircase down to the edge of the river. No Declan waiting there for her. No one there at all.

Suddenly, it occurred to her that Declan might not have been the one who'd sent the e-mail message.

Veering toward Artillery Park, Grace broke into a run, but she only got a few steps before what felt like a pulsing current charged through her body, causing her to light up with violent pain. Her muscles contracted, and a sudden vertigo she'd never before experienced dropped her to the pavement where she flopped around like a fish reeled in from the Mississippi.

"Don't get up on my account, Grace." Jill Westerfield stepped out of the fog, holding what looked like a gun in her hand. "Oh, that's right. You can't."

Even dazed, Grace finally knew it all. She tried

to speak, to say so, but all that came from her mouth was drool.

Jill Westerfield was Naomi Larkin transformed.

Grace had outted her, Corbett had gotten her fired, and now she was back for revenge.

WHEN GRACE DIDN'T return his call, Declan became concerned. He tried both her phones again, but she didn't pick up.

He didn't want to worry her mother, but what choice did he have? Luckily, Sandra Broussard's number was listed. Declan placed the call and sweated out every ring.

"Broussard residence," came a male voice.

"Corbett?"

"Who is this?"

"Declan McKenna. Is Grace there?"

"No, she already left."

His gut tightened. "To go where?"

"Wherever it is you asked her to meet you."

"I didn't ask her to meet me anywhere." Declan tried to control his growing panic. "I told her I would call, but Grace isn't answering either of her phones."

"Wait a minute, your e-mail said you wanted to meet her at ten o'clock."

A sick feeling shuddered through Declan and he gripped his cell hard. "Corbett, I didn't send Grace an e-mail. The blackmailer must have spoofed my address. Are you sure she didn't say where she was supposed to meet me?"

"I'm positive. Wait—Minny dropped her off. Stay on the line. I'll call her from my cell."

Declan's insides knotted and twisted as Corbett made the call. Cell to his ear, he left the office and locked the door. Waiting outside for direction, he held his breath.

If anything happened to Grace, it would be his fault, Declan thought.

...I call on my faerie blood and my powers as a witch to give yers only sorrow in love, for should they act on their feelings, they will put their loved ones in mortal danger...

A McKenna couldn't escape the witch's curse. When Bergeron had died, Declan had mistakenly thought the danger was past, that he and Grace had somehow defeated their destiny. Now he knew—the moment he met her, he should've run in the other direction to keep her safe. He was destined to repeat the mistake of his father and all the other McKennas who thought they could cheat death somehow.

Guilt rushed through him, leaving him light-headed and heart-heavy. What had he done?

What had he done!

Suddenly Grace's brother was back on the line.

"Minny left Grace off in the French Quarter," Corbett said. "Grace thinks you're going to be on the Moonwalk behind Café du Monde near the steps down to the water…right now, as a matter of fact."

Declan was already running toward Decatur. "I can be there in a couple minutes. Get me backup!"

"Will do!"

Declan flipped his cell closed and shoved it in his pocket.

He only hoped those few minutes were enough to save Grace's life.

THOUGH DAZED AND DISORIENTED, Grace could still hear her attacker jabbering at her.

"After you and your brother got through with me, I had no job, no money," Naomi-Jill said. "And then came Hurricane Katrina. I was stuck in one of those horrible centers. No food, no water, but plenty of danger, especially for a woman. A gang cornered me. I tried fighting them off and was beaten so badly my face needed reconstructive surgery."

So that's how she'd changed her looks, Grace thought. Her brain was clearing, but she was unable to make her limbs do what she wanted.

"S-sorry," Grace slurred, surprised at the weird sound of her own voice.

She got a glimpse of the other woman, who was stooping now, and pulling something from the gun.

Grace focused and saw two wires that went from the muzzle to her body…and gathered Naomi was removing a cartridge from a stun gun.

"They took me to a hospital in Mississippi," Naomi went on. "After I recuperated, I learned to live in poverty. My reputation was ruined and I couldn't get so much as a job interview with any reputable newspaper or television station. I did all kinds of low-level jobs for years. The way I kept myself sane…was to plot my revenge."

Sane? Did she really believe that? Grace wondered.

Naomi was concentrating on the stun gun now, loading it with another cartridge. So she could shoot Grace again?

Grace was starting to feel her limbs—obviously the effect of the stun didn't last. She had to distract the woman, keep her talking.

"Jill Westerfield," Grace forced out, sounding a little less weird. "Who?"

"A reporter. I met her in Mississippi, became friends with her. I knew she was coming to New Orleans on business and followed her here. She was as stupid as you, following directions to come out here on the Moonwalk late at night. Yes, I had something on her, too, enough to make her do something foolish. Oh, in case you're interested, she's dead now. I did what I had to. Now killing *you* will be a pleasure."

Grace covertly tested herself. She didn't want

Naomi to know the effects were wearing off, not yet. But she could move her toes and fingers, though not completely the way she needed to.

"Laroche…" she gritted out. "Part of this?"

"Not that he knows. I seduced him and convinced him to hire me as a publicist so I could get to you and Corbett. I wanted to take everything from you as everything was taken from me. I found a kindred soul in Bergeron Prejean. It didn't take much to convince him to help me."

And he was able to bully Eula into giving him access to the studio dressing room, Grace knew.

"Kill him?" Grace mumbled.

"I couldn't have any witnesses. So far it was the only part of my plan that went the way I imagined. I wanted to leave you Broussards stripped of your reputations in addition to your money. I was just getting started. But now I see the error of my ways and I know what I have to do. I'm putting a new plan in place."

Naomi stood and aimed the stun gun at Grace.

But before she could pull the trigger, a voice came out of the fog from behind her. "Sorry to spoil your plan."

Naomi started and whipped around and even as Declan stepped forward, she aimed and shot off the second cartridge.

Horrified, Grace watched helplessly from the

ground as Declan shouted, his body dancing before he dropped to the ground, one arm and shoulder hanging over the first step leading down to the water.

"Now I have to kill you, too!" Naomi shrieked.

Chapter Nineteen

Stun gun still in hand, Naomi got on the steps behind Declan and tugged at his body. His muscles spasmed. Nothing he could do to help himself, Grace knew. He went down…down…down toward the storm-tossed waters. Trying not to panic, Grace gathered her strength and pulled herself along the pavement, crawling toward them. She had to do something before the crazed woman drowned the man she loved!

Her head was clearer now, and everything seemed to be working, if at a low level. Grace pushed herself into a sitting position. She willed the world to stop moving around her and somehow got up on shaky legs. Unsteady on her feet, she rocked where she stood and gauged the distance to the steps. Naomi was halfway to the waterline and possessed with unnatural strength as she dragged a helpless Declan with her.

"Naomi, stop!" Grace shouted, stumbling forward.

With a screeched "You bitch!" the other woman gave a big tug on Declan before letting go.

As he slid down closer to the river, Naomi reached in her pocket. When she pulled out her hand, she connected what she had taken from the pocket with the stun gun. Grace realized she was loading a third cartridge.

"No!" Grace screamed, stumbling forward and throwing herself off the walkway to stop Naomi before she could shoot the damn thing again.

Grace slammed into the woman and the stun gun flew off into the water. They stumbled off-center together and hit the chain that swung between posts. Naomi tripped and fell on her back. Grace landed on her. Preparing herself for a fight, she realized Naomi was unconscious and must have hit her head on one of the big chunky rocks scattered along the bank.

Hearing a groan, she turned to see Declan sprawled over the stairs, head down toward the waters that rolled up over the bank, over his head, threatening to drown him. His limbs thrashed, but he obviously had no control over his body yet. Panic made her move fast. She kicked away from Naomi to free herself from the other woman, but as she did so, Naomi started rolling down toward the river's edge.

Grace tried to grab the woman to keep her from going in, but the waters of the Mississippi reached up for the murderess and sucked her straight into the current.

Unwilling to let the same thing happen to

Declan, Grace scrambled to the steps and collapsed next to him. Desperate to save him, she pulled his head free of the water. His eyes were open and he was trying to talk.

"Save your strength," she said as sirens and flashing lights and excited voices signaled the arrival of backup. "It's over, Declan. And we're both still alive."

"COME HOME WITH US, Grace," Sandra Broussard said, fussing over her daughter an hour later as the medics locked up the ambulance.

Grace hugged her mother tightly. "The medic said I'm all right. That Declan and I will both be fine. Being stunned didn't cause any permanent damage or long-term effects to our muscles or nerves."

The scene was surreal, Declan thought, keeping his distance as he had since being half carried to the ambulance by a uniformed policeman.

The fog lingered in drifts and puffs, haloing the lights not only of the ambulance, but also of the half dozen responding police cars. They'd been poked and prodded and had given their statements. A police boat was on its way to search the river for Naomi Larkin.

Rather for her body.

Declan could pin the moment the life had been snuffed from the crazed woman—her emotions had flatlined along with her heart—and it hadn't happened in the water. When she'd landed on the rocks, either her neck had broken or her head had cracked open. Or both. Not that he would tell Grace. She didn't need to know for sure. She didn't need the guilt.

He had enough guilt for them both.

Tonight had been the scariest night of his life—he'd almost lost Grace—but she was still alive, and that's all that mattered to him.

"I just want to know you're safe," Sandra was saying.

"Sorry, Mama, but I'll be safe with Declan," Grace said, gazing at him with wide-open eyes and heart. "I need to be with him now."

Declan shook his head. "Go home with her, Grace," he said, trying to ignore the soft feelings cocooning him, trying to trick him into believing they'd outrun the curse. "Go be with your family. They're the ones who need you now." With them, she would stay safe.

"You can try to push me away all you want, Declan McKenna, but I'm not having any of it this time. You're stuck with me." Grace hugged and kissed her mother and then her brother. "I'm so sorry it turned out this way, Corbett."

"You were right about Jill…about Naomi all along," Corbett said, voice tight. "I'm just relieved you weren't hurt. If you had been, it would have been my fault." Her brother kissed the top of Grace's head and looked at Declan. "Thank you for taking care of her."

Declan clenched his jaw and didn't say anything. Corbett's despair covered him like a shroud, informing Declan that the man grieved for the woman who'd tried to kill his sister. Grace escorted her mother and brother to Corbett's car, hugged them again, then jogged back to him.

"I'll take you home," Declan said, wrapping an arm around Grace's shoulders, perhaps the last time he would touch her this way. No matter what she said, he knew what he had to do. "We'll have to get a taxi." Which meant they would have to walk over to Decatur.

"You do want to be with me tonight, don't you?" Grace asked as they started off.

"You know I do…but I honestly don't know why you would want to be with me."

Grace poked him in the ribs. "Maybe because I care about you and don't want to be without you."

"But I let you down."

She stopped dead in her tracks. "When?"

Declan nodded to the river. "Out there. You could have been killed."

"I *would* have died if you hadn't shown up. Naomi was going to Taser me a second time and then dump me into the river."

"Instead, I let her Taser me and you had to save me."

"Is that the problem?" Turning into him, she reached up and touched his face. "That I saved you in return for all that you've done for me? Would you rather I had let you die?"

Heat shot through him at the full frontal contact, but Declan stopped himself from taking Grace in his arms. "No, of course not."

"Then stop complaining."

"Grace, we can't be together. Surely you can see that."

"Why not? Bergeron and Naomi are gone for good." She lifted her eyebrows and almost smiled. "If they come back to haunt us, I know some people in the French Quarter who can take care of that."

"Go ahead and make light of it. But I know what I know."

"And I know what *I* know. If half the things I've seen in our future come to pass," Grace said, rubbing up against him, "we're going to be so happy together you'll forget there ever was a prophecy."

Steeling himself against seduction, Declan shook his head. "I have to leave. I have to do what's best for you."

"*You're* what's best for me. I believe that with all my heart. And if you leave, I'll follow you. You were right—I'm not like Lila. I love you, and there's nowhere you can hide from me."

"You love me?"

She nodded and ran her hand down his chest. "So you see, it's too late to be noble, because wherever you go, I'll find you. I've learned a few things about investigative techniques in the past several days."

Wanting to be swayed, he couldn't help one last protest. "Grace—"

"Declan! It's time you learned to trust yourself. Trust us. Together, we can make it. Bad things happen to everyone. Maybe not this bad. Or maybe terrible in other ways. Injuries and illnesses that have nothing to do with prophecies or curses. Whatever is out there for us, we'll survive. Tell me you want that for us."

"I want to believe it with every fiber of my being."

"Then kiss me," she murmured.

He took her mouth in a sweet, drawn-out kiss, and the New Orleans night suddenly came alive.

The Mississippi River crashing into the shore and the tortured melody of a saxophone filling the air along with the smell of fried oysters and beignets and chicory coffee. The hot, humid air clung to his skin…the woman who heated him to his very core, who was everything to him and had cast a spell over him just like a real Voodoo Woman.

"I love you, Grace Broussard."

"Then take me home and prove it."

* * * * *

*Harlequin Intrigue top author Delores Fossen
presents a brand-new series of breathtaking
romantic suspense!*
TEXAS MATERNITY: HOSTAGES
*The first installment available May 2010:
THE BABY'S GUARDIAN*

Shaw cursed and hooked his arm around Sabrina.

Despite the urgency that the deadly gunfire created, he tried to be careful with her, and he took the brunt of the fall when he pulled her to the ground. His shoulder hit hard, but he held on tight to his gun so that it wouldn't be jarred from his hand.

Shaw didn't stop there. He crawled over Sabrina, sheltering her pregnant belly with his body, and he came up ready to return fire.

This was obviously a situation he'd wanted to avoid at all cost. He didn't want his baby in the middle of a fight with these armed fugitives, but when they fired that shot, they'd left him no choice. Now, the trick was to get Sabrina safely out of there.

"Get down," someone on the SWAT team yelled from the roof of the adjacent building.

Shaw did. He dropped lower, covering Sabrina as best he could.

There was another shot, but this one came from

a rifleman on the SWAT team. Shaw didn't look up, but he heard the sound of glass being blown apart.

The shots continued, all coming from his men, which meant it might be time to try to get Sabrina to better cover. Shaw glanced at the front of the building.

So that Sabrina's pregnant belly wouldn't be smashed against the ground, Shaw eased off her and moved her to a sitting position so that her back was against the brick wall. They were close. Too close. And face-to-face.

He found himself staring right into those sea-green eyes.

How will Shaw get Sabrina out?
Follow the daring rescue and the heartbreaking
aftermath in THE BABY'S GUARDIAN by
Delores Fossen,
available May 2010 from Harlequin Intrigue.

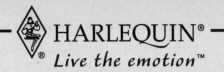

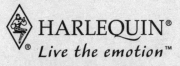

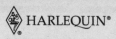

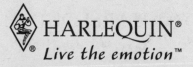

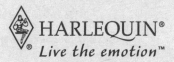

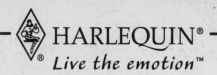